PROTECT & SERVE:
II
EXODUS

Within a year's time the Mcgurt Family became an household name and a force to be reckoned with. Under press's orchestration, the four amigos all became mulit-millionionares. The Mcgurt Family Cartel (MFC) managed to make more money then they could imagaine. The family hustle reinforced an accurate manisfestaion of Press's prediction. Press delivered on his promise. And this was reassuring to Flores who was now reaping the benifits of his investment. Flores was one of the most respected and feared men of Columbia. He was a South American drug-lord. He was so impressed with the MFC'S performance that he decided to discount the price of the pure cocaine which was imported from South America. The cost per key declined from fourteen stacks to ten five per sq. Now, thanks to press, the MFC was the new distribution center for more than two-hundred kilos. The economy ran on supply and demad and there was a huge demand for the MFC'S top of the line product.

Eve's territory was Savannah's Southside, while her workers distributed large parts of cocaine on the west side. Ace controlled East Savannah and the Thunder Bolt area, while Tandra, the queen-pin mom, found her comforts on the outskirt of the city. The center of her domain was Pooler and Richmond hill.

Press moved his queen in the spot where Noble drew ali placed his rook. As time passed the dynamic duo's friendship continued to grow more and more. The old man was now playing an active role in press's life. Noble drew ali was embraced by the MFC. Now he was being treated like extended family. Those competitive chest matches were still held. But now, the tables had turned and Noble drew ali was victor-less to his protegee and constantly borrowing money.

"You do realize that you haven't won a game since we sat down? Let me find out that you're a pain freak," Press teased.

Ignoring press's sarcasm, Noble drew ali made the next move.

"So. What are you going to do about Eve?"

"Don't kno' what you talkin' bout."

"Son. I might be old. But I'm not deaf. Or blind."

"So you heard a few rumors. So have I. Don't mean shit."

"If you say so press. This organization just doesn't need anything unwarranted."

Eve had finally found her niche, splurgin. Now, she was lit, club hopping, and boisterous, to say the least. Eve's behavior was so flamboyant that it drew the attention of the federal bearu of investigations. Press received word from Officer Daniels, who was now a sergeant and dear friend. Sergeant Daniels was press's eyes and ears within the eleventh circuit. The word around the bearu was that the MFC members were the only blacks in the state of Georgia with a steady supply of cocaine, coming directly from Columbia.

Press threatened to suspend Eve's access to the product upon his discovery. She was instructed to keep a low profile until the federal investigation was over. But Eve's behavioral conduct wasn't anyone's business, including Noble drew ali's, in press's eyes. Ali was like family true enough. But punishing Eve would cause conflict amongst the remaining MFC members who would certainly come to Eve's aid, which would crumble the empire from the inside and press just wasn't prepared to let that happen.

"You know press. I'll be honest with you because you're like a son to me. Flores is going to get rid of her if he feels like she's a liability"

"*Fuck Flores*. Again. Hearsay doesn't mean shit. I told you she's good, didn't I?"

Silence

"Now. Set the chest board up and stop lusting over my cousin ol' man. She's too old for you."

◆ ◆ ◆

Eve pulled up to the white building that was located inside of Forsyth Park's parking lot. Hopping out of a lime green Lamborghini, she checked her make up to make sure that her shit was intact. The sleepless nights were starting to catch up with her so her facial accessories were starting to become more and more of a necessity.

Entering the building, Eve headed towards the crew of camera men. They were all set up and waiting on her, the executive producer. The small studio was clinically bright on set. To the rear of the room there was a chair. Next to that sat dildos, vibrators, condoms, and a few pieces of colorful lingerie. There was also pictures of Marcus Garvey and Jesse Jackson hanging from the wall. But Eve made all of her employees take them down in haste creating a huge ruckus. The office space was currently being leased for two thousand dollars a month therefore it was a place of business and not an African American museum. This was her justification for her anti pro-black rant.

Everyone had said that Eve was ludicrous for partaking in her latest investment, *Evangelist*, a Independent pornographic film company. But Eve could care less about the opinion of the naysayers. It was her money, so she'd spend it how and when she pleased. Besides, it wasn't like she was starring in the movies herself. Although she had to admit she got turn on from watching. Ever since Eve was young she had a fascination with the adult film industry.

"Rite there. Perfect. Now in this next scène you're going to fuck her doggy style", Eve coached as the inspiring actor, her employee, Brad, removed his shaft away from his co-worker's vagina. Then the camera men changed angles in an attempt to capture the facial expressions of the inspiring amateur pornstars.

Fed up with the girl's performance, Eve nearly lost her temper. "Uuuhh. Lil girl. For the thousandth time, look into the camera. Shit. Do we need to put this on instagram live? Because your not this shy when I see you post. I know you can make more noise than that slim Kardashian. This is an adult film. Not a library."

Eve still wasn't satisfied even though slim Kardashian took the advice and followed her orders.

"B. Slow down some and let her lay flat on her stomach. Don't look into the camera. Focus on your stroke. We're trying to make a hardcore flick here and you not fucking her good enough," Eve complained.

In the middle of the next sex scene, Eve's phone rang. She answered irritably, not taking her eyes off the two performers.

"Uuhhh. Lil bra. Wad'up?"

"Shit. Those actors working your nerves again? I can hear it in your voice?"

"U alreadie kno lil bra. So wad'up?"

"Coolin'. You went shopping yet?"

"Unt-un. You need clothes already? I just gave you some."

"You know how I do big sis. Gotta stay fresh," Vlad bragged.

"Aiight. I'll go to the mall once I'm done here. I'll text you," Eve promised, prior to ending the phone call. She was impressed with her young boy Vlad's drive. She had just given him a key of cocaine not even three days ago and already he needed to re-up.

After hurricane Katrina, the young boy relocated to Savannah Ga and now he was proving to be her greatest asset.

He's been working hard for months. He deserves a promotion

Resuming her role as CEO and executive producer, Eve repositioned her attention to the film's production. She was disgusted. Her frustration with today's performers knew no boundaries.

"Not again Brad. Wtf?"

"I don't know what's wrong boss lady. I probably need some more Viagra. And pills."

"Pills my ass. You're pathetic. You've been doing this a lot lately and I'm sick of your shit."

"Now you know you my nigga and all but I'll fire your ass if I have too. My movies were hardcore, consistent, and marketable way before you came into the picture. So you need to get your shit together if you want to continue to have a leading role in my films."

After the speech Eve gathered up all her employees and demanded their attention.

"Aiight Everyone. Time is of an essence and we need to put the finishing touches on this production. But we're going to wrap it up early today. You can thank Mr. Tender dick over here later."

Following this brief speech the camera men started putting all the equipment away in haste. The two up and coming actors already had their clothes on by now.

"Oh, and B. This weekend, bring a hard dick. I don't care where you have to get one from, but you better have one. I heard you like to get your nose dirty, Pinocchio. You aint foolin nobody. Aligning yourself with that softball is going to cost you your job, especially if that alignment happens during filming. One more strike and you're out," Eve threatened, imitatiting a baseball umpire as she threw on a two day old pair of Gucci shades.

Following these words, Eve exited the building. Hopping into her quarter million-dollar Lamborghini, she picked up the phone and dialed Press's number.

Now, it was time to go shoppin.

CHAPTER 28

Paranormal activity

For the past year Aundrea and press had become insep-arable. In the beginning, press thought that Aundrea was just another dope boy's groupie, praying on trappers. But her personality & personal preference proved him wrong. Aundrea had become an African American community leader and activist for prison reform.

As an adopted child, Aundrea had it rough growing up. Both of her real parents were killed, and her oldest brother was serving a life sentence. The only remaining family member that she had was a younger brother, and he was heading astray already at an early age. Because of her lack of direction, Aundrea turned to the streets, doing anyone or anything to make a living. After com-mitting a string of crimes, she finally got busted for forging bad checks, which lead to her losing custody of her young brother, and a three-year prison bid.

But that was then. Now Aundrea was a fateful church member and civil rights activist. Not to mention press's fiancée.

"C'mere babie. I'm so happy that we're pregnant. Seems like we been trying forever. C'mon. She's kicking. Touch my stom-ach."

"You mean he's kicking," press corrected as he massaged and rubbed Aundrea's big belly.

"How many times do I have to tell you that it's not going to be a boy? Stop jinxing my baby," Aundrea teased, poking press's chest playfully.

"Since you want a boy, and I want a girl, maybe we'll have a hermaphrodite."

"Half a dyke? Speak for yourself."

"No, hermaphrodite, silly lol. It's when someone is born with both male and female sex organs."

"Really? Now I know where the saying "go fuck yourself" originated."

"You so silly."

Aundrea pulled out a white sheet of paper an studied it.

"Remember that good time bill that I was telling you about? This is it right here. I'm thinking about using it during my next speech."

The couple had a brief conversation about Aundrea's upcoming speech. Then she layed her head down on press's chest, gently rubbing his pec's, and massaging his left arm.

"Bae. You know you getting bags under your eyes? You need to get some rest," Aundrea chastised.

After a few moments of silence, she continued. "Press. Do you really want to marry me? Be honest?"

Press responded to Aundrea's comment by thinking about the promise that she made him make. Aundrea made him promise that he'd stop hustling once they were married. But what Aundrea didn't understand was the thrill that came with the game. As a cop, press chased criminals and he felt like he signed up to make a difference. But now, he finally realized his true intentions. He liked the danger. The thrill of the uncertainty is what gave him a rush. He was a junkie for action. Life without living on the edge was no life at all. The dope game provided the same adrenaline for him as a cop and he couldn't function in society without his daily dose of action. When it came to press, it wasn't about the money. Thanks to Flores, and his convict relatives, he had more than enough. Outsmarting the *system* is what excited him. The very thought of capitalizing off of the government's ignorance brought a sense of purpose and serenity to the depth of his loins.

Press knew that he and his team members were under surveillance by the federal bureau of Investigations. Officer Daniels was responsible for informing press in advance, his longtime friend and confidant. An open investigation was ongoing and it was extremely obvious. But walking away would compromise his clientele, and pride, and backing down from a challenge wasn't a part of press's genetic makeup.

Now, Aundrea was seven months pregnant with his child. Real soon, she'd be his bride. But press wasn't sure if he could live up to the oath that he pledged. Even tho he had a bad feeling that trouble was around the corner.

CHAPTER 29

Diamonds in the rough

Captain Love looked the young thug in the face searching for a sign of weakness. Unexpectedly, he found it. Then, he played on this advantage by implementing his routine strategy for interrogation.

Looks like he's about to shit a brick. Perfect. He's scared.

"So. You apart of the MFC too now? It's what you told one of my agents. How so?"

"My sister's fiancée. Press. He's in cc—harge." The young thug stuttered, scared to death.

Captain love started clapping, encouraging everyone in the room to give the young man a round of applause. "Bravo. Just look at what we have here gentlemen. A celebrity. Anyone that's connected to the MFC is a fuckin superstar," Captain Love made fun of the kid continuously clapping.

"Does press know you out here nickel & dime'in? Three ounces of cocaine is like fuckin' peanuts to you guys, isn't it?" Captain love ask, continuing to mock and intimidate the young fellow.

After interrogating and making fun of the petrified thug, the patty wagon arrived to take him to jail. One of the narcs jumped out of an unmarked car and found three ounces of cocaine on his personnel.

For the past six months, agent love had been operating under his new status as captain. Ranger was now the Deputy Director of the CNT squad. He recommended his second in command to serve as his replacement. Now agent love was the boss of all bosses and his new-found position was solidified through the Chatham county board. But this new-found position only made him worse as a individual. As assistant director, Agent love was dangerous, powerful, and arrogant.

Captain Love tried to reach out to press on varies occasions. But press would always decline his invitation. But now, a meeting between the two was inevitable. Because press's brother-in-law was in police custody. And he was scared to death. The current circumstance had just given captain love the upper hand because press was unaware that CNT arrested his brother-in-law.

Captain love was well aware of the fact that press was now the head of a million-dollar empire. Every snitch in town was responsible for circulating this information. In the *C-pote*, keeping a low profile is almost impossible once you climbed that financial latter, especially if your in the drug trade. In a split second, any potential baller's name could ring bells, and the MFC'S name was ringing so much that it could've been a telephone.

But what made the MFC'S organization so strong was press's prior knowledge and experience in law enforcement. Press knew every trick there was. So it was next to impossible to cripple the family's legacy, or infiltrate the interior of the infamous squad.

Laughing to himself, captain love sat back in his chair. An evil grin appeared on his black face as he continued to plan the MFC'S demise.

Big shot press. Now he thinks that he's the man n shit. Punk ass. Disloyal son of a bitch. He's finished. The best part about it is that he doesn't even know it yet.

The Johnny mercer theater was located inside of Savannah's civic center. Mostly known for its performing arts, this theater was a 2,566 arena, one of the largest prosceniums in the southeastern part of Georgia. Infamous for its ability to hold large crowds, the Johnny mercer theater was a historical place. Some of the country's most influential people was credited for gracing its stage.

The chief of police looked at the size of the crowd in awe. The entire MFC had come out to support Aundrea's cause. She was holding a speaking engagement and this crowd was her biggest to date.

"The government doesn't pay taxes, we do. So our voices should have an impact stronger than it does," Aundrea said using a handkerchief to wipe the sweat that descended from her cheekbones. Walking around the stage slowly with the microphone in her right hand, Aundrea continued to recite her well-rehearsed speech.

"Where's all my convicted felons? By a show of hands, how many of you guys have been to prison?"

Two or three people raised their hands.

"Brotha's n sisters. Don't be ashamed of your past. I went to prison," Aundrea confessed, unapologetically raising her own hand.

Half of the crowd raised their hands anxiously.

"I knew it, Aundrea smiled. This is the *c-pote*. Everybody n their mama's been to prison. Literally," she teased.

"I know how it feels to come home to nothing. No job. Nobody wants to hire you. You have mouths to feed, parole fees to pay, maybe child support. I been there."

"But we have to have a sense of direction and never lose hope. The minute you forget where you come from is the minute you forget where you're heading."

"PREACH SISTAH!" Someone yelled.

"YASSS!" Someone else screamed.

Aundrea talked about the state of black America and how the

revolution was far from over. Hearing this the crowd roared in agreement, triggering Aundrea's emotions and level of confidence.

She went on to call the tea party members idiots and she voiced how Dr. Martin Luther King's dream never happened. She then spoke on mass incarceration stating that it was a civil rights issue equally important as the LGBT & Black lives matter movements.

"I just received this letter from the chairman of the United States Senate, Aundrea said enthusiastically. She held the letter up in the air and rotated it around so the entire crowd could see it. This is called a good time bill. He support's it and it was sent to congress just yesterday."

"My fellow sister's n brother's. It is our *duty* to support this bill. The federal bureau of prisons is operating at a 149% rate way over its capacity. A 10% reduction in the prison population will save taxpayers 1.2 billion per year."

"Our economic crisis is due in part to the state of our judicial system where so many offenders are given crucial sentences, but no outlet to redeem themselves. In prison, the inmates have no reason to desire rehabilitation, or work towards an early release. And we need to fix that."

"So do we want to see stiffer sentences? Or results!" Aundrea asked the crowd, the base in her voice rising.

"WE WANT RESULTS!" Multiple people screamed at once in unison.

"PREACH SISTAH!" Others yelled.

"We can change the way the system enforces punishment in a way that would benefit both the inmates and society," Aundrea added, right before exiting the stage.

Motivated, the crowd gave her a standing ovation. Aundrea was brilliant. And fearless. Much like her idol: *Rosa parks.*

After passing out her contact information, Aundrea headed

towards her awaiting family. Upon arrival, her in-laws all took turns giving her a hug and a round of applause.

"That was deep," the Chief of police said sincerely.

"Yea, I was hypnotized. You should've seen me girl. I started to join you right then and there. Especially when you started talking about Donald Trump's racist ass," Eve exclaimed.

They all took turns complimenting Aundrea and voiced that she was a gifted motivational speaker. Press, having witnessed this a million times before, was always impressed with his fiancé.

She never seizes to amaze me. Standing ovation he smiled.

The MFC was big contributors to the black community. Recreational centers were built, donations were made to several churches, and professional tutors were assigned to assist the underachieved children that dwelt in the urban community. Even the homeless people reeked the benefits of the MFC'S generosity. They were the *real* humanitarians. During holidays, they were each required to do community service. Press, Aundrea, and Tandra always passed out food. While Ace & Eve were summoned to spend quality time with some of the handicap children. Surprisingly, Press stood firm on his promise. Press was giving back to the community so much that some nonprofit organizations started to hate. With every passing minute nosey citizens told that the MFC'S sponsorship in the inner city was encouraged by drug money, which didn't fall on deaf ears. This information was reported to the city council members. But press could care less about the political gossip. He never even denied the allegations.

Yup. I'm helping my people using dope money. And? At least I'm trying. You nonprofit corporations don't do shit for the community but steal.

Press looked up at Aundrea who was currently having a conversation with his dad. She was beautiful. Bold. And Charismatic. She was definitely a diamond in the rough. She was born in this world with so little, yet she overcame so much. And the more Press looked at the size of the crowd, the more he realized just how lucky he was to have her in his life.

CHAPTER 30

Revenge is LOVE

Pulling up to the abandoned warehouse, Press made sure that he had the right directions. Yup, this was it he figured. He could tell by glancing at the glossy beamer that sat right beside of him. Its appearance and features hadn't changed one bit since the last time he remembered seeing it.

Pissed, Press slammed his hand repeatedly against his oak wood steering wheel. It had been hours since the last time that he had spoken to Aundrea, his girl for the last year. He left text messages and called everyone that she knew but no one seemed to have any idea about her whereabouts. These facts lead Press to come to one conclusion, and one conclusion only: She was a cheating.

"Now here I am about to go to war for "her" brother and this is the thanks I get? She usually works at the clothing store until closing time. Then, she stops for bible study. Later she prepares for one of those ratchet ass seminars. My biggest mistake was trusting her. Just last week, she held her biggest conference to-date. And we were so happy. What happened? Activist my ass. That bitch's a THOT."

Entering the building with this in mind, Press found the stairway the way he was instructed to. As he entered the room his stomach almost collapsed. Three rats were lying dead in the middle of the floor. The rotten smell surrounded the entire room, not sparing a single nostril. Besides the rats, and the clock that stood in the center of the room, antique spider-webs and two deflated stools were the only visible things. The clock looked outdated and it kept making an awful ticking sound.

"WAT," Press blurted upon his arrival.

"Really bro? Is that how you talk to an ol'friend? We're supposed to be better than that champ."

"I don't have all day." Press spat, never breaking eye contact with captain love. He never removed his hands from off of his gun.

"Why are you so hostile bro? Your brotha n law isn't a priority? Maybe he is. Maybe he's smart enough to know that close mouths don't get fed," Captain love smiled.

Not seeing a change in press's demeanor, Captain Love ceased all laughter.

"Look press. Me and u go way back. So I'll make sure that my agents don't come to court. Then the state will have to drop the charges."

"I don't need yo' help, judas. Just make sure your agents are present. Because my lawyers will be."

"You know press, captain love replied, ignoring press's sarcasm. I always thought that you & I were friends. Guess I was wrong. You ungrateful sonovabitch. I made you."

"Is that so?"

"Very. Press. Why do u think I handpicked you over those officers? Not because I thought you were cute, I'll tell you that much. That day, when we searched ol'girls house, & you found that dope, I knew u were dirty. I just knew it. I sensed that you were a criminal the very first day I met u. All that holier than thou shit was just a gimmick"

"See you in court, judas," press repeated, as he prepared to leave.

Still ignoring press's hostility, captain love continued.

"The way I see it, you need eyes press. And who in law enforcement has bigger eyes than mine?"

Silence.

"I'm the captain now. I took Rangers place. I know u heard. Together, we can OWN this city press. Just you, and me."

"Put yo'pride to the side and think press. The feds are watching you. But I have a partner who works with them motherfuckers, and he knows people. People that'll turn the other cheek for the right price. It's all about politics, and the benjamin's," Captain Love tried his best to explain.

Staring Captain Love down, Press clutched the pistol that was inside of his pocket tighter. Then he chose his words carefully and precisely.

"You pussie, that's what you are. You admire us dope boys. You wanna be like me so bad don't'chu? But u can't, because you don't have the balls too. So stop lying and hiding behind that punk'ass'badge. *Coward.*"

"What do you call someone that'll take someone to jail, but mimick their behavior? A hypocrite, a low down, backstabbing hypocrite. That's what you are. A dead man walking. Pig. FUCC'U!!"

"NO FUCC'U!!!!" Captain Love yelled. You think just because you build a few churches that you better than me? So you judging me now mothafucka? I hope'not. News flash. You sell dope, you fuckin'idiot. DOPE. Giving a few homeless people sandwiches don't make you'a'saint. You're not part of the solution. You're part of the GODDAM PROBLEM!"

"I'm the fuckin'police! U know who dope boys fear? ME, THAT'S WHO! I' RUN DE BOMBACLOT STREET!" Captain Love yelled using a jamaican accent and beating on his chest like king kong.

Silence.

They both had to regain their sanity before anyone spoke again.

"You do know that I have to take u down?" Captain Love informed upon calming down. The temperature in the room was now a thousand degrees, matching the tension between the two.

"And you do know that you're a dead man if you ever come near my family again?" Press threatened.

"Matter of fact," Press added as he pulled out his formerly hidden pistol. Anxiously, He pointed it towards captain love's forehead.

"You do realize that you'll get the death penalty for murdering a cop don't chu? I don't think u got the balls to pull-dat-dere-tigger-boy," captain love spat in his most southern accent imitating a redneck unfazed by the threat on his life.

"Who said you were a cop?" Press replied questionably as he cocked the pistol back forcing the loading clip to transfer into the chamber.

Then he fired his gun and walked away like nothing even happened.

CHAPTER 31

Revelations

Aundrea still hadn't shown up when the next day arrived. Press hadn't seen or heard from her. This fact was making him madder and madder. Aundrea's absence was like a death blow to his ego because he had taken on the role of her chaperone and confidant for more than a year now.

She probably skipped town with some nigga. Fuck her. And the unborn child. Mufucka probably aint mine anyway. But why am I trippin? This isn't a vacation. I'm like Bruce Wayne, I'm rich. I built the MFC. Hell, I am the MFC. I could have Miss America If I wanted too.

Mashing the relax button, press adjusted the feel to his fifty-thousand-dollar man chair. Then he enjoyed the sounds of his small movie theater as he awaited his cousin's arrival.

An hour and a half later, Ace was grabbing some champagne out of press's refrigerator. He arrived and voiced that he was thristy and sober.

Press thought about telling his cousin about Aundrea's infidelity. But he decided against it. He'd never hear the end of it if he did. Besides, Ace was like a pregnant woman whose water just broke: *he couldn't hold water.*

"Where's Aundrea?" Ace asked as soon as he joined press on a nearby recliner. Press was watching paid in full. Rico had just killed Mitch.

"The store probably," press lied.

"Probably? Either she's at the store or she's not? Let me find out your GPS is broke."

"What the fuck's so important that you couldn't tell me over the phone?" Press switched subjects because his cousin's sense of humor was becoming aggravating.

"Guess who got fired Friday?"

"Noow," press said in shock using that *C-pote* slang, immediately knowing exactly whom Ace was referencing.

"Yup. Heard she was messing with stinkie."

"Who?"

"Stinkie. You know Stinkie. Monkey time n em's cousin."

"Anyone named Monkey time needs to be slapped, lol."

They both laughed at press's comment.

"Lol. Heard he got her on pills n all type of shit. Heard Mr. Hill, one of her coworkers, Snitched," Ace informed, as he slowly sipped from his glass of champagne. Then Ace sat his glass down on the table and lit up a swisher cigarello. It contained marijuana.

"Yup. He caught them kissing at some restaurant."

"And they fired her for that? Hill couldn't prove that," press defended. Then he thought about it.

"Unless"....

"*He took pictures*," they said in unison.

After this realization subsided, press was silent. His facial expression was full of disbelief and disappointment.

"Yup. She's a certified slut now. Stinkie done turned her out. I wonder why she was so uptight when yall were together?" Ace instigated.

"I see you got jokes. So, wad' up? You trying to re up or what? because I don't need you calling me once I get in my bed," press said again continuing to lie. Sleep wasn't an option he was just tired of Ace making fun of him.

Ace needed five bricks. He still had five, but normally he kept ten on deck at all times.

After serving Ace, press bided his cousin farewell and headed towards his bedroom. Once there, he got dressed and made plans to stop by his auto body paint shop before he went to re up with Flores.

Ace's revelation would weigh heavy on press's mind for hours. Out of all people he would've never thought that Charlotte would mess with a dope boy, let alone pop pills. What was this world coming too?

Press thought about Aundrea again and what Charlotte had thought about her on a personal level. Charlotte felt like Aundrea was a two-dollar whore who was just after press's money. The fact that he chose to date one of her ex parolees was tacky and disloyal. These were just some of the things that charlotte would share with Ace knowing that he'd run and tell his cousin.

Personally, press hadn't seen or heard from Charlotte in almost two years. At first, he thought that charlotte was just jealous of his and Aundrea's relationship. But given his newfound predicament, namely Aundrea's absence, and infidelity, charlotte was absolutely right about her suspicion. Aundrea wanted the military experience. Press was her recruiter and nothing more than a faze. Aundrea strategically signed up to be a soldier, collected her paycheck, and went AWOL.

Press opened the door of his SUV truck. He hopped out at a cheetah's pace. After checking on his employees, and doing inventory, he sat in the parking lot of his auto body paint shop. The shop was huge. He punched Flores's number in on his iPhone. It was the first number listed on his speed dial.

After ending the brief call, press prepared to pull off. He looked to the front of his window shield and noticed some trash. He dismissed the notion of removing it himself because he hadn't noticed it prior to climbing back inside the vehicle.

Press spotted a local crack head nearby. He signaled him over with his hand. He already crunk the engine up and he didn't see the need in hopping back out of the luxury vehicle.

"Aye, speedy. You'll throw that piece of paper in the trash fa' me? *Preciate it,*" Press requested pointing to the window shield.

On the way to the trash can, speedy, the smoker, opened up the piece of paper praying that it was a winning lottery ticket.

Shit. I need some luck. Or better yet a hit. He has to brake me off. He's shining too. I kno he got it. Nothing's free around this mother-fucker. Not even sanitation.

But to the fiend's surprise, it was a note. After reviewing it at great lengths, the smoker ran back to the SUV in haste. Press nearly pulled off during this occurrence.

"STOP! STOP! STOP!" The smoker yelled, placing himself directly in front of the truck.

Coming to a halt, press rolled down the window and grabbed the piece of speculative trash that was handed to him by Mr. nothing's for free.

What the fuck's wrong with him?

Apprehensively, press reached for the letter. Then he proceeded to read.

I GOT YOUR BITCH. FOR 500K U CAN HAVE HER BACK. MEET ME @ 530 IN EAST SAVANNAH ON UTAH STR. MAKE SURE U WEAR YELLOW. AND U BET NOT WEAR ANY PANTS. COME ALONE.

PS

If I see any sign of the police, she's a dead bitch

Confused, press pulled off in a hurry leaving Mr. nothing's for free to bite the dust.

But what about my hit?

The crack head asked the rear end of press's SUV as he fell down to his knees in a complete state of disbelief.

CHAPTER 32

Karma

Pulling his SUV up to the designated area, press brought a custom-made suit case filled with 500k. He did everything that the kidnapper instructed him to do in order to ensure the safety of his fiancé an unborn child. Press called his cousins and explained everything prior to his arrival, including the fact that he had to do this alone, specifically at the kidnapper's request. This revelation was met with an abundance of opposition. But press wasn't willing to jeopardize the well-being of his family. It was because of him that Aundrea was in this situation, so he'd save her, even if it costed him his own life. Some people die to live. But press was the type of man that lived to die. Especially for those that he loved.

Draped in yellow, press walked around the corner after handing some random smoker the keys to his truck. The smoker approached his SUV requesting that he head to the third abandoned house located two streets further which was near a dead end.

After following the smoker's instructions, press knocked on the specified door. Thereafter, he was summoned in by two suspicious men wearing matching masks and DRACO'S. After being searched thoroughly, and having the suitcase that he brought along removed, press was forcefully ordered inside of a small room down the hall.

Once press entered the room, his heart dropped. Aundrea was hog-tied to a chair. Duct tape covered her mouth and a blind fold was wrapped around her eyes. You could still see the dried-up tears from where she had been crying.

"Put the money down and stand ova there," a third man pointed. He too wore a mask. He was the one in charge press figured.

By this time the other two mask men had joined the trio. The shot caller whispered something inside of one of the men's ear who left immediately and went inside of another room. Then a million thoughts started to run across press's mind. Things were just spiraling out of control.

He's probably going to get something to untie her with. About time.

"Aundrea. Everything's gonna be aiight. Baby it's me. I go-

"Shut the fuck up! The shot caller yelled, still holding the suitcase that his men handed over just seconds ago. The shot caller had it in his hands. He was excited about the 500k that was secured safely inside of the brief case.

Within seconds, the other assailant returned with a gigantic plastic bag in his hands.

Walking towards Aundrea, press tried to comfort her but he was slapped with the butt of a shiny forty caliber Glock. Instinctively, he grabbed the side of this head where he had been struck with the pistol. Press was in a horrendous predicament. His forehead was partially busted.

"Did I say move PIG? Do you need a hearing aid? Next time Imma kill yo simple ass. Keep thinking its a game. NOW BACK IN DA CORNA & FACE THE WALL!" The shot caller demanded.

After a couple of minutes of silence, one of the gunmen started making fun of press's predicament.

"Is this your girl fam? Please tell me it isn't? Because this rite here, the gunmen said pointing at Aundrea's vagina. This belongs to us now."

"Head was weak," the other gunmen complained.

"Shiiid me. She knows how to perform. Super head over there

needs a Grammy. I need to rape bitches more often," the mask man bragged.

Then they started laughing.

"Both of you mufuckas shut up and hand me that bag. RIGHT NOW." The shot caller ordered.

Press, however just couldn't understand the motive behind this stunt. Something wasn't making sense in his mind, which was racing one hundred miles per hour.

"C'mon fellas. Yall said bring 500k, and that's exactly what I did. I gave yall the money, no questions. We had a deal. Keep me if you want. Just let my girl go. Please."

"If I have to tell you to shut up one more time boi. And I'on give a fuck wat I promised you PIG. 911 is a joke. Didn't your mom teach you to respect your elders? Now. Shut. The. Fuck. UP!!!" The shot caller yelled, waving his gun in the process which was mimicking his every word.

After following directions, and reaching inside of the giganic bag, one of the gun men closed it in haste. He was disgusted.

"You trippin bros. That's some gay shit right there man. Homosexuality don't run in my blood," the gun man complained in an outright state of refusal.

"Ok. Bet. Los? you wanna make 50k? Murk this bitch ass nigga right now," the shot caller barked, promising one of the goons 50 stacks to murder his own homeboy for failing to follow instructions.

Rethinking his stance, and trying to avoid Los's wrath, Mr. anti-homo (MAH) did as he was instructed. Los was known to kill for less so this truth inspired MAH'S sudden change of heart and a deeper appreciation for life. Hesitant, MAH reached inside of the bag again but this time he pulled out a plastic dildo penis. At least twelve inches long and thick.

"That's some homophobic shit rite dea," Mr. anti-homo continued to complain as he handed the shot caller the massive plastic dildo.

Finally realizing what was going on, press swung on the shot caller with all his might, grazing him across the jaw twice. Press fought with every fiber in his body. But his strength was no match for the forty caliber, which jerked and shot him three times in the chest.

Hit in both the chest and his stomach, press continued to fight. But he was outnumbered and no match for such manpower. The two other goons rushed him, punching him directly in the pupils of his eye ball sockets.

Out of breath, press caught a brief glimpse of the tattoo that the shot caller sported. During the confrontation and commotion, the shot caller accidently left that part of his skin unattended. It read *MR. EAT ME.*

"HOL HIS MUCKIN ARMS DOWN," Mr. EAT ME ordered as press continued to rebel. He was unwillingly detained and handcuffed.

After suffering from yet another beating, Mr. EAT ME shoved the plastic dildo up press's buttocks with all his strength. Up and down it went, from side to side, matching the rhythm of a rollercoaster.

"Now keep still. You been fuckin niggas for years, now it's my turn. You like taking people to jail and digging inside of their butt cracks don't chu? C'mon. Admit it. The feeling is mutual. Pig," Mr. Eat me mocked as he inserted the dildo in and out. He performed this method for what seemed like an eternity, until there was no more strength left inside of press to fight with.

Having sustained multiple gunshot wounds, right above his abdomen, press was helpless. All he could do at that point was pray that the assailants put a bullet inside of his head. At least then maybe he could leave this earth with some dignity and a small fraction of his manhood.

But Mr. EAT ME was enjoying the slow torture too much to honor press's wishes.

"Wat did u say? I can't hear you RuPaul. Wat's that? Do it harder? My pleasure."

Mr. EAT ME continued to mock the way that press was screaming as he rammed the plastic dildo as hard as he could until it reached press's insides. This event not only tore up press's insides but it caused a very disturbing and intensified bowl movement.

After the intrusion, press was bleeding like crazy. Both his head and his buttocks was bust wide open and covered in red. His yellow outfit was also red and he was seconds away from becoming unconscious.

Disgusted, Mr. anti-homo and Los left the room, leaving Mr. Eat me alone with both press & Aundrea. But unbeknownst to Mr. anti-homo, the offer that Mr. Eat me had made earlier still stood, and Los had every intention on cashing in on that extra 50k.

"Look at me," Mr. Eat Me said to press, now pointing his forty caliber at the center of Aundrea's forehead. After hearing press's painful cries, her dried up tears were replaced by fresh ones. She now had a face full of tears and she couldn't stop shaking her head.

"I said look at me or I'mma take dat same bloody dick and FUC HER IN THE ASS!" Mr. Eat me threatened, the base of his voice rising. Mr. Eat me was still mad despite receiving the money and embarrassing press enough already.

Once Mr. eat me saw that he had press's attention, he fired the gun, twice, huffing and puffing in the process.

Satisfied, he grabbed the suitcase full of money and exited the room. The other two men awaited patiently for his arrival in a nearby van.

It seemed impossible for press to lift himself up. But somehow he managed. It took everything that he had inside of him. Crawling towards aundrea, press fell back to the ground. It felt like she was miles away from him instead of a few feet.

After a brief struggle, press finally made it to his destination. There, aundrea was slumped over with two six-inch hoes stapled to the middle of her forehead. Fresh blood oozed its way down her face, piercing through the blind fold which was still covering her eyes.

Crying hysterically, press crawled onto the top of aundrea's dead body. The impact from the gun knocked the chair that she was still tied to down.

"AUNDREA! AUNDREA! WAKE UP! DON'T DIE ON ME! PLEASE BABY! I NEED U! AUUNDREA! AUNDREEEEEEA!!!!" Press cried, not realizing that it was too late. Aundrea was dead. The reaper had dialed her number a long time ago.

Asking god why, press fell unconsciously on the peak of aundrea's stomach, smothering their unborn child.

In the blink of an eye three lives were destroyed. Just that quick.

CHAPTER 33

Retaliation is a must

Exactly a week later, press was released from memorial's hospital. Having been treated from severe burns and multiple gunshot wounds, press was still hurt badly, both physically and mentally. He just couldn't accept the fact that Aundrea's was a victim of homicide and she wasn't coming back. Ever.

"Pappi. Don't worry. Ju just get better," Flores encouraged using his Columbian accent. Him and Noble drew ali had come to press's mansion to discuss the tragedy. This was the first time that they could talk in private since the incident.

During press's stay at the hospital he was visited by a slew of people. But the MFC members were the only visitors with unlimited access. News reporters were parked outside of his hospital room begging for an exclusive interview despite the fact that he was recovering and could barely pronounce a proper sentence.

"Our hitmen are the most reliable professionals this country has ever seen, Flores promised. With the information that you just provided us, we'll find him. You just make sure that you take care of our guy once he does his job. Grease his palm and I promise you there will be no worries my friend."

"Ju do realize however that our conversation has to remain a secret, especially given the nature of your previous profession. This doesn't leave the room. Understand?"

Press nodded, reassuring Flores, as he did in the past, that the conversation would remain confidential. Flores apologized for what happened to Aundrea again and then he departed. But not before promising press to personally contact the organization's most treacherous hit man within the southern region.

Noble drew ali was extremely concerned about press's mental state of mind and he made sure to expressed this verbally. Then finally, after being reassured that press was ok for the millionth time, Noble drew ali left. His parental paranoia was in overdrive. He left two armed guards as security, despite receiving a high volume of protests from press, someone he had grown to love as if it were his very own son.

Shortly thereafter press received a call from sabastian's new attorney, Daniel Scottie. According to Scottie, he needed press to come to court to recant his statements as a witness now that sabastian's appeal had finally come. The only problem for press was that the trial would last that entire week. Not wanting to go back on his promise, press asked scottie to postpone the trial until he was through grieving aundrea's death. But scottie said that press's request was impossible. Scottie also said that it would be disastrous because sabastian would lose trial again if press didn't show up for court to testify. At that point, press wasn't sure what he'd do. His only concern was grieving in peace and attending the funeral.

Thinking about his family, press didn't realize how overprotective they were. They practically went ballistic after Ace and Eve found him nearly dead and unconscious in that abandoned house. After telling his cousin's what street that he was headed to before having his phone removed, they rounded up a whole army of goons, disregarding his instructions. Press had told his twin cousin's not to worry about him and the only reason that he was calling in the first place was to let them know where he stashed all of his millions just in case he died.

After interrogating everybody in East Savannah, Ace and Eve was approached by the same random smoker who approached press. The kidnappers offered him, the fiend, an ounce of dope if he did as he was instructed. But the trio of goons failed to keep their end of the bargain, according to the smoker. Once the deed was done, so were they. They left in a dark green van and they all had on black. That's what the smoker admitted to telling the cops verbatim.

Pissed, the Chief of police issued out and all-out manhunt for whoever was responsible. Every cop, citizen and goon within the region was looking for that green van. Ace and Eve was offering 500k to anyone who could provide any information about what took place. They also insisted that they keep press's company even though they all had stayed with him at the hospital. After a long fight, and a lot of profanity, they finally agreed to let press go home alone. Although press was extremely appreciative for his family's love, he wanted to grieve the death of Aundrea and his unborn child without any interference and distractions.

Press thought about what he was going to do to the coward who murdered aundrea and his unborn child. That day, in the midst of all the scuffling that took place, he noticed the leader's tattoo that read: Mr. Eat me. It was the same tattoo that the guy had a long time ago when agent love forced him to search the guy's buttocks for dope back when press was a rookie narcotics agent. It all made sense. That's why Mr. eat me was so mad. Because press was the sole reason he went to prison.

After digging up some old arrest records, Flores was able to gather some crucial information concerning Mr. eat me's true identity. According to Flores, the *UAT* operated in silence, and so did its branch of hitmen. There were literally thousands to choose from. But press wanted the best of the best.

It was also said via Flores that The *UAT'S* hitmen were known as the American Assassination Association, aka TRIPLE A. Each leader was given authority over thousands of members from each coast and there was a total of five leaders. The leader that press hired represented the southern district.

The life expectancy for Mr. eat me became shorter with the factor in the above paragraph. A bloody revenge was set to take place, thanks to a grieving fiancé, with a misplaced soul.

Aundrea's funeral was packed to its mass capacity. So much so that the chief of police brought extra security to the funeral to minimize any potential outbreak that would happen on the behalf of its attendees. There were so many people in attendance that the graveyard site could've been mistaking for a club. Aundrea's influence reached thousands and everyone had come out to pay their respects to someone who had been so instrumental and influential in the community.

The chief of police watched closely as the pallbearers lowered the casket six feet deep. He couldn't even imagine what his son was going through. A few days prior, during Aundrea's wake ceremony, press snapped, after seeing her disfigured face for the first time since she was killed. Her slim facial structure was now the size of a bowling ball, encrusted with two matching bullet holes. It was originally supposed to be a close casket ceremony. But press demanded to see her face anyway. He only snapped after witnessing the result.

Press was becoming a maniac. It seemed like the more that reality was setting in that aundrea wasn't coming back, the more psychotic he became. Press was no longer the righteous son that the Chief and clarissa had raised. Unapologetically, he closed down the doors to all the MFC community centers. He even reneged on his promise to donate funds to charity, for no apparent reason, other than the obvious. Now, trauma was press's best friend. It was an artistic masterpiece composed by none other than Mr. Eat me, aka Picasso. This was press's defining moment. Because no love remained inside of his cold heart: *Only anger.*

"Are we talking about the same chick? Dark-skin? Slim? You better not be playing us," agent Mendez threatened. He was now second in command and negotiating with a potential CI (confidential informant).

"I could say the same. Matterfact. Since we talking trust, I want to see this agreement in writing." the CI rebutted.

"I never made a deal with you."

Narcotic agent Mendez started rubbing his chin in a state of curiosity.

"Ok. Just so we're clear. Your going to give up her location? And wear a wire? What's this? Christmas?"

The CI sat down and kicked his feet up on the desk. His new bargaining strategy had given him an edge and he was enjoying this power.

He shook his head.

"My uncle's in prison and I'm looking to extend my services in exchange for a sentence reduction."

"Not possible." agent Mendez countered.

"That's not what *he* said. *You* promised me," the CI said now addressing captain love directly as soon as he walked into the room. In return captain love reassured him that he'd honor his request despite overriding his partner.

"I'll be supportive when I hear that audio. You just make sure you get a confession."

"You just worry about keeping yo end of the bargain. That support does include those nine ounces of cocaine we discussed too, right?"

"Maybe. But remember, this deal in its entirety is contingent on your ability to deliver. Bring me that audio."

After the deal was concealed, captain love was left by himself inside of his organic office. He smiled to himself at the thought of the deal that he just made and how press's days as a free man was numbered.

Rubbing the back of his neck, captain love cursed out loud. The pain was excruciating. Thanks to the leader of the MFC, his ex-partner, his skin had to be patched together with stiches sur- gically. He checked into memorial's hospital shortly after the incident. Press shot the old clock that was right above his head, and a few pieces of glass fell, which grazed his neck and small portions of his scalp.

At this point Captain love felt like he had to redeem himself. But not just because of his injury and current predicament.

You owe me. You ungrateful son of a bitch

If captain love could have it his way, he'd physically assault press in person. But he knew that press was under the protec- tion of *UAT,* even from a hospital bed. There, it was rumored to be a series of security guards. Captain love found out about Aundrea's kidnapping the same way everyone else did, via social media. He actually reached out to the MFC and sent his condol- ences. After all, Him and the CEO were once partners so he felt as tho that was something that press didn't deserve. However, this tragedy wouldn't change the dynamics of this feud. The streets were run by either the cops or the criminals. The hogs, or the pigs. If one was not a member of the law enforcement fraternity, or an ally of the CNT's division, then you were considered an enemy, and press had choosen the latter. Press's decision would come back to haunt the MFC in due time. The plan of his demise was already underway.

CHAPTER 34

Menace too, society

Press sat in the VIP section of the club while sipping his patron drink. A few years back, him and Charlotte partied at this spot. They got so drunk that night that they had to be escorted out by security for disrespecting the owner. Press remembered it like it was just yesterday because he was fond of those memories. This is what brought him back to this paticular club.

Both of press's security guards were nearby, monitoring the crowd. Just a few hours before, him & Eve had been hanging out together. She had come to press's house and demanded that he have some fun and stop moping around. Aundrea died six months ago and she would've wanted press to celebrate life and not dwell on the past. This is what Eve said in order to convince press to go out. She delivered the request of Aundrea's dead spirit.

After eve kept bugging press, he finally agreed, and they hung out for a while. But Eve didn't stay long. One of her workers, Vlad, needed to reup so she had to take off after a brief stay. One of the security guards that NDA assigned to press kept inquiring about Eve's whereabouts. This line of questioning created a sense of hysteria and suspicion.

Did she promise this man a starring role in one of her adult films like she did everyone else? Is she fucking him too? Press wondered.

Having not been out in a while, press in took his surroundings. He needed some "poonanie." He hadn't had sex in weeks. The club's crowd was normal tonight. Not to pack. Or over-crowed. And that's exactly how he liked it.

"Let me buy you a drink," Press whispered in this fine Latino's ear once he hit the dance floor.

"I'm sorry. But I don't take anything from strangers," the girl flirted.

"My bad. I'm Preston," Press greeted, extending his right hand.

"Isabella."

"Nice to meet you Isabella. Ok. Now can I buy you a drink?"

"Your funny. You sure don't give up easily do you?"

"Nope. So. What you drinking?" Press persisted.

They walked to the bar and grabbed a couple of drinks. After they left the bar, they danced for a few songs. They were having a good time but things got awkward once they were joined by a third party. The woman just walked up and gave press a hug, pushing Isabella to the side.

"What are you doing here? Press asked with a Kool aid smile.

"I was about to ask you the same thing," third party responded rolling her eyes at Isabella."

"Can we talk? Privately?" third party asked.

After press asked Isabella to excuse them for a second, she sucked her teeth and started to pout. But press was too focused to care and occupied with Ms. third party's company. Now she had all of his undivided attention.

Once they made it back to the VIP section in a quiet corner, the woman hugged press again this time for a longer period of time.

"I heard what happened press. I'm sorry. I tried to make it to the funeral," Third party explained.

They talked for hours. They caught each other up on everything for old time sake. She told him how she met the dope boy out of sandfly and how he tricked her into popping molly pills.

She told him how she got terminated from her job. Now she was working at Piggly wigglys and living with her parents.

Press didn't know why but the woman's honesty meant something special to him. He didn't even plan on bringing what Ace had told him up. She volunteered this information and that alone suggested that she still trusted him, even though so much time had lapsed since the last time they spoke. He missed the intimate conversations and being in her presence. A broad smile arose on his face for the first time since that tragic day that Aundrea was killed.

Tonight, Press's drought would definitely come to an end. And every other night too thanks to his first love, and ex-girlfriend, Charlotte.

◆ ◆ ◆

Menace took the cocaine from out of the sofa bed and placed it on a digital scale. It read 25.3 grams, the plastic screen read. Its revelation was not only shocking but also an insult. Menace was someone that had a bad temper and zero tolerance for bullshit.

These shits short again? Conniving ass plug. Out of 10 bricks, none of them' weighed up. I got sumthin' for his bitch' ass.

Menace also thought about his status and how he himself suffered from a robbery, having just bounced back not long ago. Three years ago, his livelihood was literally snatched away from him by the woman infamously known as Eve. In Menaces's opinion, Eve was conniving and shady. They had met at a club where they became friends, which led to casual sex, and eventually a full-blown relationship. She moved to Charleston, South Carolina, just to be with him. Menace always knew that she was from Georgia, but he never knew what part, although the two of them was a couple for nearly five years.

One day, after a long fight, Eve called the police on him. So, like any man with half a brain would, he left, leaving the drugs, money, and drama behind in haste. When he did return, Eve was gone, and so was the 30 bricks that he had buried in his backyard. Surprisingly to him, Eve even had the combination to his safe. This safe stored two hundred thousand.

Eve very seldom spoke about her family so Menace didn't know anything about them. At least not until now. In the process of running some errands, he managed to run into someone who just happened to bring her name up during a conversation, which intrigued his curiosity, and lead to some very revealing dialog between him and the guy. According to this source, he was really close to Eve. He had also boasted that she was living in Savannah Georgia, balling & spending money with a passion, and an unlimited budget. Eve was the executive producer of the films that she financed. She was the owner of a successful adult film company the guy bragged.

After getting to know the guy a little more, and boldly offering him 100k, which was a 50% increase from where he originally placed the bounty on her head. Menace felt as tho a ton of bricks was lifted off his shoulders. He was shocked that eve's so-called friend would sell her out that easy. The guy was disloyal in his book But he made sure that his facial expression didn't give his true feelings away.

Eve was a snake in Menaces's opinion. She lived up to her birth name. Any female that cause's a shorter life span for billions of people' cannot be trusted.

God evicted Eve from the garden of Eden. Her entanglements with the serpent made him livid. As the saying goes, every dog has his day, including female ones. Spectators were plotting on Eve from every direction. Her good luck charm had finally run its course. Because not only was she on the FEDS radar, she was also on Menaces's. He hated her guts with a passion and he was disgusted with her selfishness and blatant disloyalty. This new information made him vent and self evaluate.

So you buying porn companies n shit with my money bitch? Really? You gone' need a "Evangelist" after I'm done with yo' ass. You backstabbin, baldheadit black bitch. I swear to god, no bitch steals from me and gets away with it. No bitch!

CHAPTER 35

Idols become Rivals

"How's the investigation going on the Mcgurts? The FBI deputy director asked from behind his six-foot desk. He just hung up the phone and was expecting the two federal agents.

"Not good. He's smart," Federal agent Ruscoft informed shaking his head.

"What about the others? I'm sure you guys must've gathered something by now?"

"We have a confidential informant that's willing to testify on Eve Mcgurt. Problem is, the CI says the drugs that he did score from her were in very small quantities," FBI agent Millsap explained.

"And even if we relied on our informant, this happened over a period of time. If we grab her now we'll compromise this whole investigation," Millsap protested.

Agent Ruscoft interjected. Yeah cap. Once they realize that we're on to them, they'll shut down the operation. Especially Preston."

"Well we're going to have to make a move soon. We've been investigating the Mcgurt family for two years now and we still don't have a fucking clue how much drugs they're acquiring."

"But cap. W-

"NO FUCKIN BUT'S RUSCOFT. The clock is ticking and I need answers. Comprend'e?"

"The mayor is fuckin pissed because the chief of police's son is supplying the fuckin city and he thinks that the chief and I are somehow protecting him. Now I don't give a fuck how the two of you bird brains have to accomplish this, but get it done," he threatened.

"NowgetthefuckOUT!!!" The FBI deputy director yelled.

Walking out of the office, federal agent Ruscoft and Millsap mumbled to themselves. Who the hell did cap think he was talking too? FBI agents were the best at their jobs. Didn't cap understand that Preston mcgurt was a fuckin cop previously? Press knew all the tricks before they were even pulled out the bag so of course the MFC would be a tough organization to infiltrate.

Federal agents Millsap and Ruscoft had been following the MFC for almost two years and they knew everything there was to know about them individually. Eve was into adult porn. Press owned a few clothing stores and an auto body paint shop. Tandra and Ace owned several restaurants and small portions of real estate downtown. They even knew that Press and Charlotte reconciled, and that happened not even a week ago.

The FBI took pictures and interrogated employee's all while listening to the word on the streets. But besides that they had nothing. Nothing substantial enough to crumble the empire. They needed to put the pressure on a family member. They needed to find more friends, side pieces, and in-laws. What they needed was the weakest link: *And they had the perfect person in mind.*

◆ ◆ ◆

Eve raised her skirt, and panties, granting her protee'e, B, access to her vagina. Sometimes, she had a little meaningless fun with her employee. They were currently sitting next to one another in a business meeting and a few of the shareholders were voicing their concerns and objections. The 2nd largest shareholder (Eve was the majority) currently had the floor.

"We can make use of Amazon Web Services to lower costs substantially," the shareholder continued. But the entire operation, will be automated, with most of the hosting on a Amazon server."

Searching for confirmation, the group looked to Eve for answers. But she was breathing heavy and seemingly oblivious.

Eve took another incredibly slow sip from a nearby cup that was filled with coffee. Then she rolled her eyes.

"Up front the first hurdle is convincing Visa or MasterCard to let us accept payments. Still, that's not the hard part guys."

"If we calculate it in hours spent on developing the software ourselves, we're looking at around 3 months. We'll say it takes 500 hours, approximatey. We'll charge $65/hr if we have to take on freelance clients, which means we're looking at about 32k for someone within our rate."

A few of the other shareholders also shared their opinions. This happened following Eve's rebuttal.

When *she* was ready she gave her presentation.

"Here's the technical stats: The site iself runs on a single server, a VM actually. It runs PHP with Codeigniter for the framework and MySQL as the database. And trust me when I say our technican will make extensive use of the Codeigniter's caching abilties."

"We'll have an FTP server setup where the usernames and passwords are powered by MySQL. Each studio gets their own FTP login. We're currently in the process of acquiring a cronjob that will run every few minutes and pick up files that upload after gathering some basic meta information and sending them to Amazon S3."

"Once the video is safely on S3, the studios can complete the meta data, pricing, and choose when the video goes live."

Eve was then given a round of applause by all of the board of directors.

"Gentlemen. New shareholders. Welcome aboard. Behold. Our goal in five years: 753 studios 19,138 videos, and Apx 5000 visits per day."

The board members gave eve another round of applause. Even the shareholder who had reservations participated.

After conveying her speech, eve removed Brad's finger from inbetween her legs. Now that she had everyone's undived attention, she wanted to capitalize.

Mmm

"Now. Here's the new direction for this company:

"Close your eyes. Picture a beautiful woman, scantily clad in some red lace lingerie. Picture her batting her eyes flirtatiously, then slowly making her way over to you."

"But this is not a flesh and blood women. It's a three-dimensional performer in a 360-degree immersive video and she is so convincing that you can barely tell the difference. Virtual reality is going to be huge and we're ahead of the curb. We will unlimitedly allow consumers to pursue their wildest sexual fantasies."

"See gentlemen, by 2025, such adult content is forecast to be apart of a $1 billon business. It will be the third-biggest virtual reality sector, after videogames and NFL-related content. It's the next mega tech theme in the US, akin to the mobile-phone industry that happened 15 years ago."

"E-toys, which will make a huge impact digitally, and be an extension of Evangelist, will sell for $99 apiece. It'll be commanded based on on-screen action in real time. The films will be pre-programmed, with software developers synchronizing toys and content in post-production, similar to the way filmmakers add subtitles to Hollywood films."

One of the shareholders interjected. He thought the current pornography climate is where the focus should be, on films using real people, in real time.

Eve looked at the guy who made the comment in disgust. She disliked his objections. And suit.

"Blah blah blah, she laughed, motioning her hands as if she was snapping her fingers.

"They'll be enough money for everyone, relax. One hundred and ninety-three billion in revenue is predicted by 2023. That means our time is now. On a global scale, each smartphone user of adult content is expected to watch an average of three hundred and forty eight videos this year, with the biggest growth expected to occur in the US where video views will grow by almost 55%."

Eve excused everyone dismissively following her speech. Even her star protegee. He was getting on her last nerve and being too aggressive.

Brad wasn't anyone that eve could see herself dating. He was another one of her boy toys. Fun. But not hubby material. Lately, he had been acting real sneaky and shady. First, there was the rumor about him sniffing cocaine. And now, he was making off the wall comments during business meetings.

Brad was actually the shareholder that complained and presented objections. Long story short, the previous shareholder died, leaving brad, the pornstar, in charge over his will and portion of the company. Rumors leaked saying that the shareholder and brad were practicing homosexuality, which inspired the transfer of shares and massive estate.

I gotta keep an eye on him. Dick good and all. But he not worth it. Too aggressive. And overprotective. He's trying to replace me as CEO. I can feel it.

For the next couple of weeks Press and Charlotte were inseparable. They rediscovered what was lost and recaptured the bond that they desperately missed among one another. Press felt bad about his feelings for Charlotte, especially so quick after Aundrea's death. Ultimately, he realized that he was still in love with Charlotte despite having a dead fiance.

Press and Charlotte did everything together. They shopped, clubbed, fished, and played the playstation. She even went with press to make drug transactions. She never questioned his intentions or judged him like before. She just accepted him for who he was and press was ecstatic about her transformation.

In no time Charlotte moved into Press's three story mansion. He even purchased her a bens of her choice, the latest model. Thinking back on his dad's words, press smiled to himself. His dad had said that this was the happiest that he had seen press since Aundrea died. He also said that him and that anchor chick wasn't together anymore because him and Press's mom, Clarissa, decided to give it another shot.

The chief tried to convince press to give the dope game up like he usually did every time they spoke. The Chief never wanted that type of lifestyle for his son epesically having witnessed his older sister self destruct for far to long.

Press thought about the dope game. The FBI was on him like white on rice. Surely they knew he recognized the undercover agents that posed as civilians. The lawn care attendant? The mail lady? His uber driver?

After all, he was an ex-cop, not a fool. Or did the FBI forget? Press felt like he was so far ahead of the FBI that they needed a time machine to catch up. They were living in the *first* century instead of the twenty-first century.

Gazing at the stars from his three-story tower, press inhaled the weed and blew the smoke out slow. He was spent after him and charlotte's sexual escapade.

Earlier, Ace called and said that he had a surprise. He spent two weeks in Atlanta on vacation and stumbled accross something special, something that would be the best gift ever according to him. Curious about Ace's enthusiasm, Press enjoyed the midnight view once more before heading inside.

Spending her Lamborghini sideways, Eve jumped back onto the talmadge bridge. She rode the interstate on the way coming back from South Carolina. They were headed home to the SEAPORT. They were leaving leaving Karma, a popular strip club, located in Hardeeville, South Carolina.

"Thanks sis. I appreciate all the support. I feel special."

"You are special," Eve encouraged.

Then she paused for a minute before she continued. "How did you like them strippers? They was thick. Especially the one that you pulled to the VIP section. What happened?"

"Nothing," Vlad blushed, embarrassed.

"Nothing my ass. Thotiana," Eve teased.

They rode in silence for two whole hours before either spoke again. For most of the ride they were on dark roads and there was not another car in sight.

"Why are you mean muggin? Eve asked, concerned.

Silence

"You were just telling me how grateful you were. Now you in your feelings. Bipolar self."

"You mad? Ok. I'll stop the stripper jokes."

"U good, Vlad waved. Just tired," he confessed while starting to yawn.

Two hours later, Eve and Vlad finally made it back to the SEAPORT. They were headed to get Vlad's birthday present. Eve promised him a gift before leaving Karma.

Eve hopped inside of her Lamborghini with a huge smile on her chocolate face. She had just come out of one of her many trap houses in the west Savannah area.

"Happy birthday. Sensitive ass," Eve smiled, handing over a plastic bag full of snowflakes.

Vlad looked at the bag of dope in awe. Up until this moment

he had never seen that much powder at one time. The whole ordeal made his eyes stretch by ten inches. But he concealed his excitement.

"Nice looking out," he thanked her.

"I want you to be in charge Vlad. That's your birthday present. I'm promoting you."

After not receiving the reaction that she was looking for the mood changed.

"You not ready to get no real money. The silence says it all."

"Sis, stop trying me."

"Just saying. It's time to be a man Vlad. When I became a man, I put away childish things," Eve preached, quoting the apostle Paul from the bible.

Then she made a right turn heading towards East Savanah. She was about to drop Vlad off to his SUV. It was near Pennsylvania avenue.

After they reached Vlad's SUV, he hopped out and headed towards his truck.

All of a sudden. Out the blue. Gun shots rang. Coming from every direction.

Shook, Eve tried her best to avoid getting hit but she was unsuccessful. She took a bullet in the shoulder blade. Squating, she opened the door of her Lamborghini. She had to put the car in reverse to get out of the deserted area.

Eve felt like her chances of survival were better on feet. She saw the man who had shot her and he looked like he was out to kill. The shooter was right beside Vlad's truck and she kept hearing gun shots. Vlad was already dead by now she figured.

Eve ran like a young Marion jones. Her adrenaline helped her to cope with the bullet wound and soothed the pain.

She was hit again. This time in the back. And again in the leg. Exhausted, eve fell on the side of an abandoned house. Vlad came to her rescue, minutes after her collapse. She was glad that he wasn't dead. She watched him hold his gun out. Searching for the assailant.

Then.

She watched as he pointed the gun towards her dying body.

Horrified, she mouthed the word nooo as Vlad closed his eyes and pulled the trigger.

CHAPTER 36

Ace boon coon

The following morning Ace pulled up to Press's mansion bright and early. Charlotte was asleep inside of the house. Now they were standing beside Ace's car making jokes and smoking a blunt.

"Still trippin on you and Charlotte. Yall talked more shit about each other then a lil bit. Just killing my poor little ears," Ace joked, playfully pulling on his earlobes.

"You heard the saying. Can't live with them. Can't live without them."

"Speak for yourself lover boy. The only thing I'm giving these hoes is second base."

"They young women cuz, not hoes."

"I meant no disrespect. I love women. Calm down Kirk Franklin."

They discussed family. Life. And Eve. Then Ace presented his gift. It was a car. A convertible.

After giving press a tour, and opening the trunk, Ace signaled press with his hands. After press saw what was inside the trunk, he thanked his cousin calmly. Then he gave him dap and told him to meet him at midnight downtown on river's street.

◆ ◆ ◆

Once midnight arrived, press headed downtown. Contemplating on whether or not he should bring a chain saw, he stared out the driver's side window. Then he made an important decision. He would do just fine with the steel baseball bat and blow torch.

For hours later, Press and Ace sat inside of his car waiting on the coast to clear. There was a drunk white couple lingering around. It took them nearly an hour to walk off. This is just how drunk they were.

Popping the trunk, Press picked up a stick and poked a man. The man was inside the trunk and Press was trying to make sure that he was still alive. After receiving confirmation, they struggled to carry the man's body together. But they finally managed to make it to the end of the strip nearing the Marriot hotel.

Hogtied, they rammed buddy's body against the rail, which was placed there for support and to protect people from falling over into the Savannah river. This was the whole purpose of the name river's street because it was home of Savannah's infamous river.

Press then slapped the man with the steel baseball bat.

"Long time no see. Now wake your bitch ass up."

Unwrapping the blind fold and duck-tape, Press watched as the man's body began to lean. His head was busted open already after just one swing.

Silence.

"O' you aint got nothin' to say? Hun? You aint happy to see me?" Press roared swinging the bat again but this time with more force.

Press chopped buddy more aggresively, longer, and harder. Ace had similar aspirations. His cousin was having all the fun.

"Cuz. Run to the car and get that blow torch. It's under the driver's seat," Press ordered.

In no time Ace returned with the blow torch. But before handing it over, he made a few jokes. Ace was a clown. This was a matter of life and death and yet he still managed to display a sense of humor.

"Bros, if I was you I wouldn't say shit either. But before you go out like scareface, let me explain. A blowtorch is a fuel-burning tool used for applying flame and heat to various applications, usually metalworking. Which means you will officially be remembered as the man of steel."

"Still wanna go out like tony Superman?" Ace instigated.

But the guy remained silent. Ace, having never witnessed this amount of courage, continued to cheer him on. He started clapping and giving a fake round of applause.

"Bravo. This guy knows he's about too die and yet he doesn't speak. That's the OG I used to know back in middle school. I wanna be like you when I grow up."

"Brillant I say, just brilliant," ace joked using a fake London accent."

He handed press a small blow torch shortly after this. Which changed the landscape of the whole silence dynamic.

"Cat still got your tongue?" Press said politely, referring to the statement as a fact more so then a interrogation. Mad, Press ignited the fire.

Before Press could even lite the fuel-burning tool correctly the guy broke the code of silence.

"Wat? You wanted me to tell you that I was finna rob the bank? So you could've tried to talk me out of doing it? Hun press? You're still mad because I chose not to answer the phone? So you could've snitched on me? You was the fuckin police press. I couldn't trust you anyw--Trick tried to explain but got stuck mid-sentence. His body began to shake prematurely and he started coughing up blood.

"I didn't think that shit was gon bring that much heat onto you. How the fuck was I suppose to know that they were going to lock you up?" Trick pleaded.

Ignoring Trick, press positioned the blow torch towards Trick's bloody skin. He lit it and pointed it at Trick's leg. The fire started penetrating through trick's leg causing him to scream.

"ACE! PLEASE MAN TELL YOUR COUSIN TO STOP! PLEASE MAN!

ACE PLEASE! I SU--------AAHHHHHH! Trick cried out for help. But there weren't any second chances or sympathy given. Trick robbed the bank without giving press a heads up and that was dishonorable.

Everything that Trick had said made perfect sense. Deep down, Press knew Trick was right. Back then he couldn't be trusted. But Trick had proven to be selfish, conniving, and disloyal, which were all ethic violations.

Press pretended like Trick was Aundrea's killer in his mind, turning up the heat. This time he sparked it onto Trick's chest.

Tired of hearing trick scream, Ace placed the duck-tape back over Trick's mouth. At this point the flames had already reached Trick's lips, barely missing Ace's fingertips.

Satisfied, they struggled again to pick up trick's body. The difference was now that his body was burning it was heavier. This weapon was truly a fuel-burning tool used for applying heat onto varies applications. The fumes coming from the ashes of Trick's burned skin was confirmation.

Finally, they managed to lift his heavy, crispy body. This task required much patience. And strength.

Together, they threw Trick's body over the rail. They heard a splashing sound on the way to their vehicles.

CHAPTER 37

Hardache and chains

"Get the fuck off of me!" Tandra yelled fighting the guards that was at memorial's hospital. After a small altercation, she was escorted to the parking lot by security.

"And what the fuck are yall lookin' at?" Tandra yelled to some innocent onlookers for no apparent reason. Tears of anger was pouring down her cheek.

Tandra left the hospital speed walking 60 miles per hour. She went crazie after her daughter was pronounced dead. This couldn't be happening she cried. This just couldn't be happening.

Eve was Tandra's best friend. The one person that she could confide in. Eve was Tandra's lifeline and her daughter didn't deserve to die in the middle of the street. Whomever did this would pay. Nobody touched a Mcgurt and lived to talk about it. All hell was about to break loose.

Charlotte signaled Tandra with her hands as they walked across the street and got into Charlotte's bens. When Tandra got the call about Eve, she was having a brand-new stereo system installed inside of her corvette. Not being able to reach none of her immediate family members, she called Charlotte, and together, they flew to memorial's hospital. She was escorted out shortly thereafter.

On the way to Tandra's house, neither said a word. The atmosphere was full of silence and vengeance. But zero conversation. Eve's death had Tandra's emotions running wild. Charlotte tried to comfort Tandra by asking her a question. But her gesture, while generous, only made it worse. "No, I don't need you to stay and baby-sit me bitch. Is your name on my lease? Does your mail come to 17 ventura blvd?"

Once they reached Tandra's house, she stormed inside. She knew that Charlotte was only trying to help. But only the strong survived and there was no sympathy for the weak. Especially within the MFC. Which was replicated, founded, and established by a council of elders, namely NDA and Press. Interference with the natural evolution of life without a justifiable cause was a ethic violation.

Dialing a certain number, Tandra waited impatiently for her gun plug to answer. Tandra always had a fascination with guns. Now that her daughter was dead, which triggered her pursuit of revenge and psychotic behavior, she could go overboard, and buy plenty weapons, without receiving any oppostion from her comrads. This time, due to the circumstances, such a large purchase would be justifiable. She remembered the time when she asked press to bring her a gun. He cursed her out afterwards. Those were the good ol 'days. Her and Eve joked about that particular time for weeks.

After ending the call, Tandra reached for the burgundy pouch that she had inside of her pants pockets. It contained nine ounces of cocaine. Finally, after a series of thinking, and searching, she realized that she left it in Charlotte's bens by accident.

Immediately, she felt guilty about it too. So much so that she started to call and give her niece in law a head's up. But then again, she didn't feel like being consoled again either. So she decided to get it back once she was through taking care of business.

"It's safe. Not like she's going to sell it to anyone. Scary ass."

Walking by Eve's picture, Tandra broke down and started crying. She grabbed the photo and promised her dead daughter that she'd avenge her no matter what.

◆ ◆ ◆

Later that night, Tandra linked up with her connect. Her artillery plug. It was almost midnight and they agreed to meet up at one of her trap houses near the Pooler area of Savannah's metropolatian.

"Miss me?" The plug greeted walking through the door with two duffle bags.

"Hae," Tandra replied very dullish. She reached inside of one the bags. Then she opened them up separately, one at a time. She did a thorough inspection.

Picking up on her caution, the plug made an attempt to lighten the mood."Dat ass is gettin phat," he complimented, slapping her on the backside playfully.

"What are we doing tonight?" He flirted.

"Please tell me you have more? These shits don't even have infrareds," Tandra complained.

"Wat? The guns?"

"No the fuckin guns."

"Boi don't waste my time like that no mo. You gon lose a customer," Tandra threatened.

This new change in attitude caused the plug to wonder.

She's usually friendlier. And flirtatious. Prolly on her period.

"Listen. You right, I usually have more. But this is all that remains of the last shipment. Shop with me this one-time sweetheart," the artilary plug convinced.

"I tell you what. Take the whole bag. Just give me what you think is fair."

"Motherfuker. Are you deaf? What part of no don't you understand? The N or the O?"

"Ok. I see how it is. That's fucked up Tandra. Don't fuckin' call me, period. We gon' see' just how deaf I am tommorow when I get those DRECOS. I'm talking hundred round drums," The plug threatened. He started pretending to stuff the guns back inside the bags knowing that she'd change her mind once she discovered that high tech guns were apart his future inventory.

Not wanting to pass on an opportunity to buy some DRECO'S, Tandra changed her mind, just like the plug had predicted.

If I'm gon' get Eve's killer I need all the artilary I can get. Specially those.

"Sit the shit down. Goddammit," Tandra complained irritably, but she finally gave in.

After the plug was compensated, he left. But as soon as he walked out men dressed in black swarmed the spot like some killer bee's on honey.

They're here. Shit. Jack boyz.

"Long time no see," a familiar voice said. They didn't even have to kick the door down because it was a set up. The familiar voice was a very tall figure, sporting two gold chains. He had a huge scar on the right side of his cheek.

"Guess I don't have to tell you that your fucked."

Immediately recongnizing captain love's face, Tandra dropped her head in a sense of regret and defeat. Right then and there she knew her life was over.

Something seemed funny with that little shit. He set me up. Poo u snitch bitch. I wish it was the jack boyz right about now. Goddammit.

Examining the frustration on Tandra's face, captain love continued.

"Behold gentlemen. It's Coca Winfrey," Captain love joked playfully, bowing his head down like he was greeting someone in Japan.

"You know you just fucked up right? You just purchased a bag full of guns, you're a convicted felon, and we have the entire conversation on audio. Sure sounds like an elbow to me. And I'm not talking about the one that's attached to your arm," captain love threatened.

Silence.

"Now. I can see to it that none of these weapons get picked up by the feds. And I'll make sure that your case stays on a state level. But your going to jail. Regardless," he promised.

After giving Tandra a few seconds to think this over, he continued. Don't make this too complicated Tandra. Don't take a rocket scientist to figure this one out. You know who I want."

Hearing this, Tandra became lightheaded and nauses because she knew what he was asking. But Tandra could care less. She was in her forties so as far as she was concerned she had lived her life already.

I'm no snitch. Especially not on my own family. Threatening me with life, punk ass. Hurry up an take a bitch to jail.

But then she thought about Eve. It wrecked her brain to think about her deceased daughter. If she went to jail, she couldn't get to whoever killed her daughter. She would probably have to attend the funeral from jail. She would have to wear shackles and hand cuffs, which wasn't an option for her right now. Tandra outright refused and chose not to attend Eve's funeral as a prisoner.

On a state level, with Tandra's money, and influence, she could easily get a bond. But if the feds stepped in she was fucked. The federal government has a 99.9% conviction rate. The FEDS stood for fools entering into domestic sentences. Anybody who's anybody know that the judicial system is overcrowded and puppeteered by the federal government .

Tandra felt conflicted with her thoughts and how this would impact her upcoming decision. She felt like she'd never betray her nephew. But by not betraying him she would be betraying her own daughter. Tandra was overwhelmed. And guilty. Of choos-

ing the latter.

But what other choice did she have?

CHAPTER 38

Casualities of war

Press and Ace hired a street team to pass out flyers in regards to eve's homicide. "The killer is still at large," the signs said. And right below those words was a photo of her face. They also recruited a team of goons. Goons that stormed around Savannah asking questions like they were the police. They basically interviewed everybody that didn't mind cooperating and threatened the one's that did. Together, they put up 700k in reward money for any tip or information regarding the circumstances of Eve's death. Back at the hospital, Tandra snapped on the doctor after being told that things weren't looking too good for her daughter. She started cursing and knocking pictures off the walls.

Tandra informed the family about Eve's death when she was in the car with charlotte on the way to the hospital. She had called Ace first, who called press, who called the chief and so forth.

"You know I was always jealous of the relationship that you guys had. Yall had a tighter bond." Ace confessed.

"Don't get me wrong Eve was everything. But she was your sister cuz, not mine. I represented a small fraction of her. You were her twin. You guys were closer. End of story."

They were in the middle of a conversation when press's phone rang. He answered on the third ring.

"Hello. Yeah, who dis? Bet. Enough said. Meet me on 31 & Jefferson."

After ending the call Ace gave press an inquiring look. Now he was curious.

"Tell me something good cuz. Was dat Eve's killer?"

"You meant somebody seeking the reward money? No luck in that area. But always remember this cuz. What goes around comes around. It's called karma. If revenge is a dish best served cold then I have a meeting with the waiter."

◆ ◆ ◆

"Sup?" Press greeted the mysterious man.

The man responded by nodding. Several moments later he shot straight to the point. The guy's attire screamed ralph lauren. He had a very conservative look and he sported nerdy glasses.

He doesn't look like a killer. Is this a joke? Imma discuss this with flores later.

Heading towards the back of his car, the guy popped the trunk. The slick way he performed this task reminded you of James bond. This mysterious man introduced himself as nobody.

"I know you wanted his mom, but she's dead. So I bought this instead," nobody said poking a little girl in her side once contents of the trunk was clearly visible. The little girl was hogtied both around her upper body and mouth. An older man layed there beside her hogtied as well.

"His daughter's the replacement," nobody explained.

"Took a while because he was locked up. Probation violation. So I waited it out."

"Now pay me my money."

Hearing this, press signaled Ace and gave him the okay to give nobody the cash filled with dollar bills in exchange for the two bodies filled with oxygen.

"It's all there," Press reassured as he watched nobody briefly scan through the bills surrounded by rubber bands. Although they had already negotiated a fixed amount on the way over, nobody didn't have a problem showing press that he didn't trust him. As far as nobody was concerned, flores was apart of the UAT, but press wasn't, and that's where the problem stood. In nobody's eyes, press was just another customer. And anyone that wasn't officially apart of their organization was considered an enemy and potential threat.

Nobody picked up the money. Within the blink of an eye, he disapperead, leaving both the car and the contents that remained inside behind.

That's a strange mufucka rite there. But I like it.

Shortly thereafter thinking this, Press took nobody's vehicle and Ace drove press's SUV. But before either one of them even had a chance to pull off Ace, rolled down the window.

"So wat' we gon' do with the little girl? There's a park around the corner?" Ace pointed.

"She's coming with us."

Shocked, Ace's movement ceased.

"Cuz. You trippin. That little girl isn't no more than 10 years old."

Slamming the drivers side's door, Press made eye contact with his cousin.

"Great. I'll keep that in mind the next time I visit my unborn child's grave."

◆ ◆ ◆

Press swung the baseball bat as hard as he could, as if he were babe ruth, clocking the "man from the trunk" (MFTT) across the head for the thousandth time. Both of the MFTT'S eyes were swollen and dam near shut. You could also see small spectrums of white meat, barely clenching on to the back of the MFTT'S head which was completely busted open. Paranoid, and Shocked, Ace watched in awe as press continued to go berserk. Press didn't waste any time releasing his frustrations. This anger intensified rapidly after the MFTT and his daughter were forced inside of an deserted warehouse.

"You do know that your not leaving here alive don't chu. That rupaul joke had me all in my feelings," Press whispered inside of the MFTT'S ear. Shortly thereafter, the sound of steel metal against human flesh was heard.

Exiting the room, Press went somewhere to clean himself up. Both the pistol and his hands were bleeding as a result of the beating.

Ace tried his best to comfort the little girl during press's absence. Her mouth was still duct taped and she was crying hysterically. Tears of shock mixed with shakes of her head were her reactions. The girl also had a bad case of the hick ups. But who could blame her? She literally watched her dad get beaten.

Feeling a need to partake in Aundrea's revenge, Ace struck the MFTT with his burner one time. Then again. Then again. And again. Then three more times. Ace felt triggered. There was only one way to avenge his cousin in law, and twin sister, and that was through violence.

Ace felt guilty for pistol whipping the little girl's dad right in front of her, especially since he was the same one reassuring her that everything would be ok. She was a good girl. And after this was over he'd take her, and her stuffed animal, missy, to get some ice cream. Her daddy had done some real bad things, Ace continued to communicate and explain.

Minutes later, Press returned with piece of a t-shirt wrapped around his right hand. He had a bag in one hand and a bottle of water in the other.

Then Ace watched as press pulled a small chainsaw. He started roaring the engine with his index finger. He let it run for three minutes before he instructed Ace to remove the duct tape from the MFTT'S mouth. He wanted to intimate and talk before assasasination.

"This is a terrific backyard chainsaw. It's battery lasts for hours. It's 10" bar can handle any small or medium-sized cutting job. It's so loud that noone will hear you scream, because you will shortly, trust and believe. At 7.2 pounds it's lightweight enough where I can use it for hours without fatigue."

Press reved the engine up louder and connected the saw part to the MFTT'S right leg. Press didn't drive the chainsaw too far tho. Just enough to inflict pain. Small particles of skin and meat flew off of his body. But despite this infliction, the MFTT didn't hint any sense of remorse. Or sound. He was practically speechless.

Silence.

Press then performed the same procedure, but this time on the other leg. The intensity from the vocal rejection increased which only made press madder.

Swiftly, press mashed the chainsaw into the man from the trunk's stomach, as soft as he could, because he actually wasn't trying to kill him. *Yet*

Finally, after many intimidation attempts, and refusals, the MFTT screamed. AAA-HH repeated a few times before he finally decided to speak.

"Yy-you still—(cough)—a—(cough)—p-ppig," the MFTT coughed, expressing no remorse for taking away press's family. The same soft inflicting process was then repeated to the chest area. Press would be responsible for this homicide by delivering slow death and torture.

Putting the chainsaw down, Press went inside of his pants and pulled out his banger. Disgusted, he pointed it at the little girl's head.

"Cuz, you trippin. That's a little girl my nigga. She don't have anything to do with this shit bro. We got this fuck nigga already cuz. We did good by aundrea and the babie. Don't shoot this lil girl cuz. That'a be some foul shit," Ace preached.

"Look at me," Press said to the MFTT, aka Mr. eat me.

Nothing.

"I said LOOK AT ME. O I SWEAR TO GOD IMMA FUCKIN KILL HER! Press threatened, redoing what was done to him. But press's intidating tactics no longer mattered because the MFTT was already dead.

Mad because Mr. Eat me died too fast, Press fired the gun, twice, point blank range. The hollow tips from the nine milli-meter caught the poor little girl right between the eyes. Beside her was missy, the stuffed animal. She had been shot in the head as well.

CHAPTER 39

Good things must come to an end

"Excuse me ma'aam. Do you mind stepping out of the vehicle?" The officer demanded. A few moments ago Charlotte was pulled over and asked to provide her license and registration.

"All this for speeding?" Charlotte defended.

"Quiet ma'am. This car fits the description of one that contain thousands of dollars in stolen merchandise."

"Now can you step out of the vehicle ma'am," The cop repeated, noticing two unmarked cars parked two streets down. The cars were both pitch black and screamed FBI.

"I'm sure this is a mistake. But it's ok. I'm not even angry. My father n law will clear up this misunderstanding. You may have heard of him. He's the chief of police."

Just then another unmarked car pulled up. Slow and precise. As if what was about to take place was pre-rehearsed. The driver of the car rolled down the window.

"Charlotte?"

"O. Hae Matt. Can you help? This guy's being an asshole," She poubted, despite telling the cop that she wasn't upset. Charlotte spent a lifetime trying to avoid confrontation by suppressing her true feelings.

"What's the problem?" Captain love asked, as he hopped out his own government vehicle. He then assured Charlotte that everything would be ok.

After the officer explained everything, captain love told Charlotte that she was free to leave, despite not receiving permission from the initial officer. The law enforcement representative was advised to dismiss the investigation, because termination would follow if the witch hunt continued.

Charlotte didn't know what captain love said to the cop. She was just grateful that he held such a powerful position. She hadn't spoken to him in years so it was good to know that they were still friends and on good terms. Concerned, Captain love took a moment to breath. He waved goodbye to the cop.

"You know Charlotte. Everyone is after Press. That probably was one of them right there. I think he was about to plant some drugs inside of your car before I arrived."

Seeing the shocked expression on Charlotte's face, he continued.

"Just to be on the safe side, I could check it out for you? Your call."

Charlotte nodded her head.

After searching the car thoroughly, Love pulled out a bur-gundudy pouch and examined it. Then he opened it up, slowly, and found nice ounces of a powdery cocaine substance.

"Thanks a lot Love. You don't have any idea how grateful I am," Charlotte confessed.

"Just regret not getting his name."

"Don't worry about it. That's my homie."

"Dat's your homie? Charlotte repeated, snapping her neck back and forth like women do. He just told you that didn't he? The planting the dope part? Your in on it too? She said very accus-ingily. You PIECE OF SHIT."

A brief struggle took place. Charlotte was defiant. And obnox-ious. But her antics weren't a match for a man's strength. One that stood 6'9.

"Sorry Charlotte. This isn't personal," captain love said sin-cerely, before wrapping the handcuff's around her wrist.

◆ ◆ ◆

Captain love made a left turn and landed on Abercorn street. After arresting Charlotte, Him, Narcotics agent Mendez, and Charlotte were on the way to his precint. They were just minutes away from this destination at this point.

After Tandra told captain love that Charlotte had nine ounces of cocaine inside of her car, because she and press had reunited recently, he contacted one of his police buddies, promising him a promotion in exchange for his assistance. The officer was game. But he still needed Charlotte's permission to search her car and thats exactly what she had giving him, her unknowing, unconscience, unlawful consent.

Captain love felt bad about taking Charlotte to jail via manipulation. After all, she was an old friend. However, he justified his actions as a means of survival. Her boyfriend was cutting his endeavors short by sowing up half the town. Press's product was stealing all the customers away from the dope boyz/CI'S that he had on his payroll. He tried to reason with him. But press just insisted on doing things the hard way, so fuck him captain love thought. The same applied for Charlotte because she was the potential spouse of the opps and thus a casulity of war.

All of a sudden captain love saw two unmarked cars swerve through the intersection. They flashed their lights signaling him to stop. He had a feeling that he knew exactly who this was. He saw the cars parked two streets down from where he arrested Charlotte. But he didn't think much of it at the time. Not wanting to cause a scene, he pulled over to the side.

Eying the federal badge, captain love watched as his predictions came into existence.

"Captain love? FBI agent Ruscoft asked. He stepped out of the vehicle, approaching the other, waving his badge in the process. We appreciate everything. And your department will be credited for assisting us in this matter. But we'll take it from here."

"We've been investigating the Mcgurt family for the past two years now. And your department will not jeopardize the integrity of our investigation."

Captain love snapped. "Hell no. She belongs to us! I connected the dots. I'm the one that found the leads. And confidential informants. You should be credited for being thieves. Lazy fucks. I'm not having it mothafucker. If the fed's want to take over MY CASE then you better bring me a warrant. Until then, she's state's property!"

"Again. Your department will not compromise the integrity of this investigation captain, FBI agent Roscoft returned calmly. Now I don't give a shit what you did, or how many informants you created. You are out of your league captain. We supersede you guys here, I don't need a warrant," FBI agent Roscoft said, losing his patience. The quick witted responses were insults and taking personal.

"Now. With or without your permission she's coming with us. Asshole. We'll be in touch."

Snatching Charlotte out of the back of captain's love's car, the FBI escorted her to their unmarked vehicle. Captain love gave them a look that could kill, accompanied by the worst profanity and various threats.

Always stealing someone's case. She's state property. Fuckin' FEDS. Nothin' but a bunch of goddam thieves

"Charlotte? Can you honestly tell me that you're willing to spend twenty years in prison for a piece of shit like Preston?" Federal agent millsap asked unbelievably. On the way to the precinct Charlotte volunteered her side of the story. The federal agents were now sitting in the interrogation room with her and they were using manipulation tactics and idle threats.

After receiving no response FBI Agent Millsap continued.

"I know you said on the ride over here that the drugs weren't yours. But who's going to take *your* word over a Captain's? Sure not a jury."

"But those weren't my drugs. Love planted those. You gotta believe me," Charlotte explained, teary eyed.

"Okay. Let's see," FBI agent Roscoft interfered. First, some cop allegedly pulled you over because your car fit the description of a stolen one, in which captain love, someone you knew since middle school, took the time to stop, and help you by convincing the cop that you didn't steal the car? You then gave him permission to search your vehicle, and he planted nine ounces of dope."

"Don't forget that the cop was his homeboi," FBI agent Millsap teased.

"Oh. And he told you that the cop was a good friend of his. Did I miss anything?" FBI agent Roscoft said sarcastically.

After letting his words sink in, he stared her in the eyes.

"Charlotte. You really don't expect a jury to believe your little fairy tale do you? Please tell me that this is a joke."

It was FBI agent Millsap's turn now.

"We know everything about your in-law's Charlotte. We even know about what just happened to Eve. Who do you think found her? She was bleeding to death. We followed her across the bridge that night. But by the time she got back in town, it was too late, because we fell a little bit behind time," Millsap explained.

"Matter of fact, that was the "*only reason*" why we weren't able to catch the shooter."

Seeing that he had her undivided attention, he kept on. Millsap knew that his revelation would encourage Charlotte to trust him.

"Look. We know that your not the one selling drugs. Your just a ex parole officer that made a few bad choices in men. But I have to be honest with you. You are being charged with those nine ounces of dope that was found inside of your car."

"The good news is that we can make everything disappear in exchange for your cooperation."

Placing her head on the desk like a child taking a nap during class, Charlotte broke down. Additional tears dropped splashing against her already wet face. She had been crying every since captain love arrested her nearly five hours ago.

Why is this happening to me? Charlotte shouted in between cries talking to noone in particular.

Charlotte adjusted her rearview mirror for the nineteenth time on the way to her destination. The FEDS decided to give her back her bens also if she complied. But for some reason she felt paranoid. It had been two days since she was asked to cooperate with the feds and she was practically on pens and needles ever since. She felt guilty for what she was about to do. But what other choice did she have? It was either her or the love of her life.

Charlotte just hoped that everyone understood why she had to go through with the plan. The night before, Charlotte and press had a long talk. He told her everything. How he threw trick's body in the Savannah river. And also how he murdered the man who killed Aundrea. He even murdered the guy's daughter he had informed, very proud of this accomplishment. But hearing the plan that press had for the near future had Charlotte feeling extremely nervous.

Just minutes before, Charlotte called Press and told him that she was bringing a friend by who supposedly wanted to make a purchase. Last night, she also mentioned the friend and press agreed to serve her.

The federal agents said that Charlotte's main objective was to record press's voice throughout the transaction. The friend wouldn't wear a wire just in case he got suspicious. She was also warned that she'd receive a lengthy prison sentence if she couldn't fufill the agreement.

Charlotte adjusted the electrical wire that was stitched to her bra. Then she spoke into the microphone to confirm the reception and make sure that the feds could hear the conversation.

Not sure if she could go through with it, she prayed silently that her father in law would forgive her for what she was about to do to his son.

◆ ◆ ◆

Press removed the sandwich bags from out of the duffle bag, placing each one on a digital scale. White powdery substances filled the bags and each bag contained an ample amount of particles.

After weighing both of the bags, Press signaled one of his security guards to make sure that they were on point. Charlotte was on the way with a friend. A friend who wanted to shop. He wanted the money. But he didn't trust her. Press's paranoia was going into overdrive.

Press actually felt bad about killing the little girl. He saw her face in his dreams every since the incident. Ace was pissed about it too. They weren't on speaking terms as a result. In fact, following the double homicide, a fist fight nearly transpired about him killing that little girl. At the time, his emotions got the best of him. He genuienly didn't plan on hurting the little girl or anything. It just happened in the heat of the moment.

Press shared this with Charlotte the night before. But instead of admitting that the girl was nine, he exaggerated her age. He was to ashamed to tell the truth and he didn't want charlotte to judge him or think that he was that heartless, even though he was. Press convinced himself that it was an eye for an eye. If his unborn child deserved death, then so did that little girl. Two wrongs don't make a right: *until shit goes left.*

The doorbell rang. Which was answered by the same security personnel.

"Hey baby," Press greeted kissing Charlotte as she strolled inside of the trap house. Even tho drug transcations were constantly done at this location it was still decadent. And luxurious.

"Who's your friend?" He inquired.

"Oh. Her. Ummm. She. h-

"I'm Sonya," the girl cut Charlotte off extending her right hand.

"You have a very nice place. Loving the pool," Sonya pointed.

"Good. Now this don't have to be so uncomfortable."

"Take off your clothes and jump in the water. Hope you can swim. This is officially your invitation."

Sonya did as she was told without any hesitation.

He doesn't trust me. He thinks I'm wearing a wire. Thank god I'm not. I would've been toast. Like your about to be bud. Your ass belongs to us after today.

After thinking this, exiting the pool, and putting her clothes back on, Sonya rejoined the couple confident that her swim would end press's suspicion. He was in the middle of wrapping up a conversatioin with charlotte, who was very quiet. And shy all of a sudden. She deliberately held her head down the entire time.

"So what can I do for you Sonya?" inquired press.

"I need three keys."

"Three keys? That's all?" He laughed. Then he instructed one of his goon's to retrieve the keys from out of a plastic bag.

"Not those kind of keys silly," Sonya laughed, surprised that her swim from earlier didn't deter his caution. The arm guard handed her three set of car keys.

"Look press. I'm good people bros, trust me. Your girl wouldn't've have brought me here if I wasn't. Your paranoid, I get it. But don't act like I didn't just swim in that pool to prove I wasn't wearing a wire," confidential informant Sonya explained in her best ghetto impersonation.

After contemplating his next move for a few minutes press made a decision.

"Put it on the table," he ordered, referring to the black suitcase full of marked money that she brought along. Happy, Sonya watched as press reached inside of the duffel bag. He took a couple sandwich bags out and sat them on the table.

"Satisfied?" he uttered.

Sonya replied with her eyes wide open ignoring his sarcasm. She dipped her finger inside of one of the bags and tasted the substance on her tongue.

"Dayuum. I know you making a killing off dis shit," she joked as her tongue instantly became numb.

After not getting the response that she was looking for, Sonya prepared to exit. She had what she came for now it was time to leave. Slowly, she picked up her packages, thanked press, hugged Charlotte, and exited the house.

After Sonya left Press tried to comfort Charlotte.

"Your stomach still hurt?"

She shook her head.

"It'll be ok. Just trust me. Aiight? I know what I'm doin," press whispered in an attempt to give Charlotte some reassurance.

They all gathered their things and prepared to exit. Press never liked staying in one spot long.

As soon as he stepped outside, he saw sirens, patrol cars, and what seemed like a million unmarked cars. The FBI, ATF and Chatham county police department was all gathered in a huddle waiting on him to come out. A skinny white man approached him with a broad smile on his face. All the other agents and officers rushed the house that he came out of.

Press watched the man as he pulled out a fresh pair of shiny handcuffs. The cop's badge read: FBI agent Roscoft.

"Presston Mccgurt. Let me say it's an honor to finally meet you son."

"Why didn't you just quit when you were ahead? Now your toast," FBI agent Roscoft antagonized.

Senior FBI agent roscoft wrapped the cuff's around press's wrist and proceeded to read him his rights. Federal agent Millsap also wanted to rub it in press's face that he made a big mistake by becoming a enemy to the law enforcement community.

"Son, you chose the wrong side of the fence," FBI agent millsap preached.

Considering all the law enforcement training that you recieved I would've thought that you'd be smarter. And inconspicuous. We exile former members that exhibit disloyal behavior and betrayal. If you want smoke with the police, just ask. We take care of our own."

CHAPTER 40

Fraternal Affairs

Captain love reached in his pockets and pulled out a Newport cigareete.

I need some fuckin' nicotine, fast. First the feds stole my case. Now this.

Captain love looked around the secluded room that was retained to interrogate officers with misconduct. He examined various pictures that hung from the wall. He saw pictures of the president Barrack Obama, Tina Turner, and Oprah Winfrey.

Confused, captain love wondered who reported him to the internal affairs this time. At the end of the day it didn't matter because his response would be the same as it was in the past whenever he was under investigation for police corruption: *he didn't know shit and he definitely didn't do shit.*

The Internal Affairs had been investigating captain love for years. But they could never seem to gather enough evidence against him that was sufficient enough to stick or stand trial. Within the inner community, love was known. So more often than not he already knew the grand jury members personally, which made it easier to navigate through the system and evade indictments.

It really didn't matter what the accusations were because cnt agent love intended to deny the claims. Yet in still, he couldn't help but wonder who ratted him out this time?

It had to be Tandra Mcgurt he figured. She left a thousand messages threatening him on his answering machine because the FEDS picked up her case. Love did everything that he could to keep it on a state level. In regards to maxiumizing his efforts, he was a man of his word. But the truth of the matter was he couldn't overpower the FEDS. Captain Love felt bad about it too because Tandra did deliver on her end. But what else could he do? He had tried his best. He wasn't capable of anything further. He extended his hand beyond its limits.

"Captain," the short bald headed man greeted interrupting love's thoughts. He was the chief of the internal affairs branch.

"My patience is starting to run real thin with you son."

"Now. This is the third time that a citizen has filed a complaint. Surely this isn't a convenience."

"So let's get down to it. Did you give any CI'S drug's in exchange for information? Drugs that were supposed to be state's evidence?"

"Sir. I honor my lawful duties and take pride in my job. I never broke any rules. Ever."

"Arrogant son of bitch aren't you."

"Excuse me," love felt insulted.

"Agent Mendez," the chief called out looking at captain love's right hand. Mendez was already in the building when he arrived.

"Let's show him what we think of arrogant cops."

Captain love was confused.

Agent Mendez Stood up and introduced himself.

"My real name is Fredrick Rodrigous. I was assigned to your department exactly eighteen months ago. I'm a undercover cop for the internal affairs division."

Feeling betrayed, captain love tried his best to choke agent mendez reaching for his throat. Agent mendez, rodrigous, or whoever he was was about to die. The incident happened so fast that the chief investigator didn't even have a chance to show love the body cam and arrest him.

Helpless, the chief investigator tried his best to restrain captain love but to no avail. So he radio'd for back up. Within seconds a half of dozen cops had the entire room surrounded. Two officers placed captain love in a choke hold. Another lit his chest with an electric taser.

Love was layed out unconscience in the backseat of a cop's car. Prison was his destination. It was where he would finally experience the trauma that he caused the dope boys. There, he'd find out that *"Love"* didn't really exist.

CHAPTER 41

The revival

Gwendelon turned the corridor with her beige coffee mug in one hand and her purse in the other. She was an assistant nurse at memorial's hospital and she was currently on the clock.

After doing a series of blood pressure checks and helping out, she was exhausted. Her late-night shift was just ending and she needed to deliver a message to nurse shelly. Shelly left her phone in the breakroom and her husband called, with a message, that Gwendelon intended to deliver.

On the search for nurse shelly, Gwendelon must've peeked in eight rooms filled with patients. Shelly usually made random checks on her patients every 30 minutes. So Gwendelon figured she'd locate her there.

After pushing another room door open, Gwendelon noticed that the curtains was pulled back slightly. Curious, she investigated further.

"WHAT THE HELL ARE YOU DOIN!" Gwendelon yelled after snatching the curtains back.

Caught off guard, nurse shelly tried to explain. "Oh. Gwen. Umm. I was just uh---checking her vital signs. Sounded like I heard her coughing."

"That's a lie LOOK'S LIKE YOU WAS CHOKING HER! Why in the hell would you want to kill one of your patients shelly? A dead one at that?"

"Gwendelon. Sweetheart, calm down. You hallucinating. You didn't see anything. I suggest you mind your business if you know what's good for you. Don't forget who trained you? Who do you think does the recommendation's around here?" Shelly threatened.

"You are looking to be a *real* nurse someday aren't you? Then mind your business. Because I can have your little job with one snap of my finger," shelly said snapping her fingers as an example.

Unfazed, gwendelon stormed out the room. But not before nurse shelly punched her in the back of the head.

They started rumbling. Tussling, biting, scratching, kicking, and doing whatever it took to injure one another. Shelly grabbed a set of scissors and swung. She missed. But Gwendelon didn't. Thanks to her small fist.

Hearing the loud commotion, at least three female nurses rushed the room. The other nurses were all male's including a doctor. Shelly got the best of gwendelon. But they both were facing termination. Right before they were both escorted out, they tried to convince the nurses to believe their versions of what happened. But the nurses's didn't know who to believe. Later, It was determined that the two would remain separated until there was a thorough investigation.

After the situation died down, nearly thirty minutes later, nurse illy stepped in to clean up the room. The two nurses managed to make a complete mess during the crusade.

Curious, nurse Illy pulled the curtain back and was shocked by what she discovered. This particular patient was on life support and for week's her machine's reading was flat lined. But now the readings were different. The machine's line kept moving up and down which was an indication of only one thing.

Panicking, nurse Illy mashed the emergency button that signaled the other nurses. Immediately she tried her best to help the patient, giving her mouth to mouth resuscitation. Encouraging the girl to breath, Illy remembered all the drama that surrounded her. Back when the girl was first shot, the girl's mother had to be escorted out of the building for being so disrespect-ful. She punched the doctor in the face. But if this mysterious girl's mom would've kept her composure she would've heard the doctor say that her daughter was in a comma, but she still had a fighting chance of survival. The chance was like one in a million. But at least there was some gravitation toward's hope.

Nurse Illy didn't know who the girl was but she must've been someone special. She had to be for two FBI agents to personally bring her to the hospital. The special agent's left shortly after not wanting to blow their cover.

If this girl survived, and beat the comma, she needed to play the lottery, because she was lucky. God must've found some type of favor in this young lady. No other explanation would suffice and be acceptable.

Within minutes, nurses and doctors came swarming the patient immediately, relieving nurse Illy of her duty. Frustrated, she watched in awe as the team tried their best to revive the young lady that seemed to be so mysterious.

CHAPTER 42

Dumb and Dummer

"WAT!" Menace screamed into his phone as he pasted the perimeter. He had just come from making a sale and he was now standing outside of his two story house.

"Say bruh. Imma need dat ya heard me," Vlad blurted.

"U deaf? Didn't I tell you to go pick out a tombstone? Zombie. Soon, we having your funeral."

"You tr—

Dial tone.

Thinking out loud, Menace stormed back and forth across his driveway impatiently.

This little nigga has some nerve. He half did the job, yet he still expect's a paycheck? He's bold. I'll say that much.

The deal was for Vlad to bring Eve alive, not dead. Menace had specifically stressed the importance of Eve's survival. He wanted to see her suffer before he murdered her face to face. This task was the center of their agreement. Menace had given Vlad twenty thousand dollars up front to perform the assassination. The remaining eighty would've been provided upon the job's completion.

The two had spoken only one time since the incident. But Vlad just kept calling, insisting that Menace was still in his pockets for eighty grand.

The conversation was still on his mind. So he sat down in deep thought.

This clown must be think it's a circus down here in Charleston. Got love for New Orleans. But dat tuff shit don't work down here. We too gutter and geechee.

Talkin bout she started shooting back. Supposedly, that's why he kilt her. Yeah rite. Fuck. Just like that, 20 stacks gone. Thanks to the fake ass version of Master P.

Thinking about the call that he had received two days ago, Menace slammed his fist into the garage door. Not only was Vlad out splurging with the money that he was given up front, But Eve was still alive.

After Vlad confirmed Eve's death, Menace called every hospital in Savannah to verify it. According to some lady by the name of shelly, Eve was now at memorial's hospital in a deep comma. The chances of her survival were like one in a million shelly had explained. But still, Menace had to be certain. So he sent one of his associates to contact shelly by given her sixty grand to finish the job, just in case Eve ever woke up.

At first, shelly kept expressing how much of a Christian she was. She also threatened to call the police if they continued with the harassment. However, after Menace wired half of the money to her bank account, tax free, her demeanor changed. Thirty thousand plus another thirty in six months. This agreement was binding, even if Eve never came out of the comma. A preacher couldn't resist such temptation. Currency is an addictive mechanism. Why else would a registered nurse agree to take pictures of someone's dead body during her routine checks?

The disappointment came when shelly called, which was two days ago. Apparantly, a scuffle took place. Some trainee got her ass beat and quit. Which lead to Eve's awakeining. But this wouldn't be possible if it wasn't for some bald-headed tramp named Gwendelon. These updates were given by Shelly, the registered nurse, and so-called Christian.

Menace thought about the different ways that he would torture Eve once he was able to catch up with her. The bitch could run, but she couldn't hide. By now he figured security would have Memorial hospital surrounded, so killing her there was not the answer. But this war was far from over.

Furthermore, the beef wasn't just about her stealing his money. Eve had stolen his heart. And as much as he'd hate to admit it, part of him still loved her. And that's why it was so important for him to see her up close personally, so he could throw his success in her face, and tell her what she missed out on before he murdered her.

Knowing Eve, she'd stop at nothing until she found out why Vlad wanted her dead. She'd also want to know what sponspors, if any, made contributions.

But Menace wasn't worried.

Menace was positive that him and Eve would cross paths again, despite this setback and failed attempt. Whenever that day arrived, menace would be ready, like tiffany haddish and pastor troy. The coma only represented a small portion of his wrath.

FBI agent Ruscoft entered the united states attorney's office. He got right to the point. It had been a week since his big bust and he was anxious to hear about the status of the Mcgurt case.

"Good morning," he greeted the representative for the government. Carmen was her name.

"Good morning," carman returned. Wasting no time, she explained.

"Look Roscoft. The reason why I called you here is because I have some bad news."

Silence

"We don't have enough evidence to convince a grand jury to indict preston."

"What the fuck do you mean you don't have enough evidence?" Roscoft said raising his voice.

"Roscoft, I know your upset. But I pr-

"No buts! He cut her off. He sold three kilo's of cocaine to an undercover agent. What the fuck are you, deaf? We got his fuckin voice on audio for god sakes."

"Roscoft I tr-

"One of my best informant's confirmed the authenticity of those fuckin drugs Carmen!" Roscoft yelled slapping the portfolio that was on her desk on the floor.

"I swear to god Carmen. If I find out that his lawyer paid you off or that your trying to protect a fuckin drug dealer I promise you your fuckin career is finished. YOU'LL BE JOINING YOUR COM-POD'RE IN A FEDERAL PEN!" FBI agent Roscoft threatened.

"First of all you don't have enough authority to send me to prison if you wanted too....Motherfucker!" Carmen screamed back. She had been patient with roscoft long enough.

"And I'm sorry to rain on your parade. But the lab results came back. And that was not cocaine," she corrected.

"But my informant s--

"Don't know shit about being an undercover agent!"

Carmen raised her voice fighting to contain her own emotions. Somehow, she managed to calm down some after cutting off his previous sentence.

"What she tasted was ammonia. They sell it at most corner stores in the urban community," she informed.

"But he made the transaction on audio Carmen. You g-

"You're a fuckin asshole roscoft, you know that? No, are you deaf? Carmen mocked. Not once did preston say anything about drug's on that tape. Unless you think the word satisfied would hold up in court? Even your smart enough to know better."

"He touched the suitcase Carmen."

"Doesn't matter if it wasn't recorded. The audio's irrelevant. Need a visual."

Silence.

Speechless, FBI agent Ruscoft got up to leave. He was disgusted.

"Now, Carmen said after she regained her composure. The best I could do is charge him with constructive possession for being a convicted felon. One of the guys that he was with had a registered gun. And preston's a felon, so he's not supposed to be around any guns. So that I can enforce."

"But, like I said earlier. We don't have enough evidence to charge him with anything else," Carmen exclaimed.

Press strutted down the hallway confident. Happy as ever, he was smiling from ear to ear. He had just come out of his lawyer's office and he was informed that the conspiracy and intent to distribute cocaine charges were being dismissed.

After being arrested, the magistrate judge denied press's petition for a bond. After two weeks of imprisonment, and a few political phone calls from his dad, the judge finally granted his request. It turned out that his dad even had a reach that extended beyond the federal agency, and press was very impressed with his father's display of power.

Exiting the Chatham county jail, and heading towards the parking lot, Press spotted Charlotte's bens. The night before his arrest, he confided in her, his on & off girlfriend for over a decade and high school sweetheart. He had told her how he murdered the guy who killed Aundrea and his unborn child.

Surprisingly, Charlotte understood press's love for Aundrea. So his retaliation methods wasn't frowned upon. Charlotte was so comfortable during the conversation that she shared a secret of her own. She broke down and told him that Captain love arrested her two days earlier. She said that the FBI took her into custody. They tried to force her to set him up. But she just couldn't do it she had told press, even tho the FBI manipulated her into agreeing to it in the beginning. Charlotte praised their union. She made a solid vow. And that promise didn't include betrayal. Charlotte stood up for her man by sharing this information and she was willing to suffer whatever consequences.

Just the fact that Charlotte wouldn't betray him, and was willing to take his place, as a federal inmate, meant that she was the one, in his mind. But press was the head of the household and he visualized the perfect getaway a little different. Not willing to sacrifice Charlotte's freedom, or his own, press came up with the perfect plan. Him and Charlotte rehearsed the plan for that entire night, until they were both exhausted and could no longer talk. But Charlotte was skeptical about the whole ordeal because if something went wrong, and their intentions were discovered, they both would be indicted by a grand jury, so that meant sacrificing her own-self in prison to avoid the head of the household's prosecution.

She finally agreed after varies unsuccessful attempts to make her reconsider. Press had given her confidence and reassurance that the plot would go undetected by the authorities. Long story short, they went to the corner store to get the ammonia the next morning, which was a key part of press's plan.

The plan worked but he didn't plan on being charged with the gun. His lawyer had just dropped that bomb on him as well. "Don't worry about the gun charge. You'll be home faster than a white Judge can sentence an African American," his lawyer bragged (arrogantly) dismissively. His lawyer was also a proud American. And black.

One man outsmarted the federal bureau of investigations. Press knew all too well that the police weren't as smart as they portrayed. The police were just as ignorant and dumb as regular civilians. Maybe even dummer.

CHAPTER 43

Uncle Tom

Today was the day of sentencing. Concerned, both of press's parents were present, the chief of police, and Clarissa. Together, they sat anxiously inside the courtroom awaiting the judge's verdict.

Federal agent roscoft and millsap were not far away. They too were impatient. Because they weren't satisfied with the government's negotiation. The deal had them upset, so much so that the mug's on their face's could've been mistaken for coffee cups.

The bailiff made the announcement for the courtroom to rise for the honorable judge. Following that, the court began the sentencing proceedings.

The Judge read the terms of press's probation and stated that press wasn't obligated to enter into a guilty plea, and also, that he could stand trial if he chose too, in which he would be judged by a jury. Then the judge examined the sheet of paper that was handed to him by his secretary. Shortly thereafter, he performed a series of other standard procedures.

"I see that you're here today to enter a guilty plea for one count of $922 (g), possession of a firearm by being a convicted felon."

Rereading the charges listed on the paper again, The judge corrected himself.

"I'm sorry. Constrictive, possession of a firearm by being a convicted felon. I see also that the government has agreed to abandoned the interstate commerce charge. Is that correct?" The judge asked.

"That's correct your honor," Carmen said.

Turning his attention back to press now, the judge continued. "You do know that your probation conditions has been violated because of this charge?"

"Yes sir."

"So how do you plead?" The judge asked.

"Guilty."

"And are you in fact guilty?"

"Yes sir."

After performing a few more standard procedures, the judge stared at press and shook his head. Disgusted, he cleared his throat and took off his reading glasses. He wanted to make eye contact with the drug dealing ex-cop that he had been hearing so much about.

"Before I sentence you Mr. mcgurt, I think we should talk. Let me start by asserting that I think you're a poor excuse for an ex officer of the law. Your behavior is unacceptable, and no amount of justification would be suitable for such treason."

"I think you owe everyone in this courtroom an apology."

Diabolically, press returned the judge's stare.

"Your right. I do your honor. I owe everyone in this courtroom an apology. I'm sorry that the American justice system is full of shit. Sorry that these prisons are funded by the national government who lie's and cheat taxpayer's out of their hard earn money through the penal system. I'm sorry that the federal correctional institution is the new plantation. And that men like you, "pussies in robes," are the modern-day slave owners. That just makes me so fuckin' mad."

"And no, your a poor excuse for a man, you gavel-holding-cocksucker. Only god can judge me because he's powerful. Your power has limitations."

"So go head, sentence me. Give me an upward departure and I'll appeal to the eleventh circuit. I'm warning you."

"Uncle Tom."

Angry, Uncle Tom's entire white face turned reddish. He was offended. And insulted. But he managed to keep his composure and maintained his professionism. At no time did he over-react during the verbal dispute.

"Mr. mcgurt, Uncle Tom said wishing he could give the ex-law enforcement representative a longer sentence. According to the sentencing commission, if Uncle Tom decided to give press an upward departure from the guideline's, he had to state for the record a legitimate reason, and he had none, this case was an open and shut case and minor in nature.

"I sentence you to twenty-eight months to serve in a federal correctional institution. Let the record show, on this tenth day of July, it was so ordered by the court."

Anxious to leave, the Judge slammed the gavel against the bench and dismissed everyone in the courtroom.

Relieved, press mumbled Imma call you to his parents as the baliff escorted him out the courtroom.

But not before giving FBI agents Roscoft and Millsap the middle finger.

Two weeks passed since the day that press was sentenced. As part of his negotiated plea with the government, press was on self-surrender, which meant that he could turn himself in by driving himself to prison. He had to turn himself in the very next day. So that night, Press and Charlotte made some private time, so they could connect spiritually, and enjoy themselves sexually.

Later on, shortly after their sexual escapade, press decided to get up and put on some clothes. This happened so fast that it startled charlotte.

"Unt-unn. Where do you think your going Mister? We're not finished," Charlotte objected.

Press had nearly reached the door at this point.

"I have an appointment. I'll be back."

"Where are you going? Charlotte repeated, pouting like a little baby. And why are you making me wait so long for my present? You promised me something special today, and I'm looking forward to that surprise."

"Fine. Go ahead, leave. That'll be u in the doghouse. Because you won't get any of this," Charlotte purred, pointing playfully at her private parts."

"You bluffin."

"Try me and see."

Playfully, press started barking. This happened sec onds after making the above comment. This forced a broad smile upon Charlotte's face, which lightened the mood a little. The humor reduced the tension, which lead to a sense of relief, and eventually, a smooth departure.

Knowing what press's surprise was already, Charlotte prepared herself mentally for press's official marriage proposal. Press was planning to ask her to marry him later tonight. Of course, Ace was still her number one resource. Even from jail. Charlotte also had a surprise. One that would change their lives forever.

In no time press made it to his destination. He was heading to the jewelry store, freidmans. This was always Charlotte's favorite when it can to those two metal commodities, gold and silver. Jewelry represented more than a material possession. It represented a spiritual and divine connection between human speices. This is a summary of what press believed.

Press was blown away by the diamonds. The huge stones had him in awe. The clarity was so clear that he could look in to it and see his own reflection.

After leaving freidmans, press noticed a little girl, not too far away. The little girl sported blue jean's, a white tank top, and multicolored beads. Lying at the tips of her long hair, which was braided, were the beads. They were clearly visible. The little girl just stood out for some reason.

"She can't be no more than twelve. She looks familiar."

Thinking theses things, press strutted to his truck by himself. He bidded his security farewell following his release. He even thought about quitting the dope game, following the completion of his prison sentence. Thanks to the existing war between the MFC and the Federal government there were too many human casualties, innocent bystanders, and untimely demises.

He shifted his thoughts to the current day. Tonight, Charlotte would be in for a huge surprise. He made reservations at a 5 star restaurant just so he could pop the question. He even paid the owner in advance to secure a performance from an international popular band during his proposal.

Press and Ace were on good terms again. Ace was locked again for violation of probation. This likelihood increased during Charlotte's absence because she was no longer his probation officer. Often, Ace called press from the Chatham county jail through Paytel, a communications company that provided value-added services to inmates, their families, and friends.

Press also maintained contact with Ace's lawyer. He was updated and briefed daily about the case's status.

Press remained loyal to his cousin this time during his incarsaration. But he opted out of visiting, because he himself was heading to prison soon, and his own experience would remind him just how unfair the guards are during visitation, and he didn't want to add on to that reminder while visiting his cousin in a correctional facility.

Charlotte, on the other hand, always did the road trips, despite traveling long distances to support her cousin-in-law. The relationship between the two grew and they remained cool despite the career change and transition. They formed a friendship that was quietly building for years.

Tandra also called from jail too. She was facing a life sentence. She, like her son, was currently locked up, using paytel. She often got mad if press couldn't make a three way call. This refusal was the source of Tandra's infuriation. She was upset and disappointed in her nephew. But Press felt like he was extending his reach as far as he could. He was just too busy with the MFC, life, and Ace's case. He wasn't capable of honoring her request. Especially since she hadn't taken his recconmandation and apologized to Charlotte like she was asked.

The daughter of Tandra was another story. Somehow Eve pulled through the coma. She was still in the hospital, slowly recovering. Press usually bought her flower's and he went to go visit her as much as he could. Apparently, the little goon that she had on her payroll, was the same one who tried to kill her. Vlad was his name. This attempted killer's name was revealed by Eve, who was still too weak to speak verbally, so she wrote it, in big bold letters. In response to eve's update, press issued a all out manhunt for anyone that would bring him Vlad's head on a platter.

Meliciously, he rubbed his hands together and thought about the perfect person for this type of professional job: Nobody.

Nearing his truck, press resumed his thoughts that he was having about Charlotte potentially becoming his wife. He wondered what was so important that she wanted to tell him? All he could come up with was that she wanted to take over his operation while he was in prison. For the past couple of weeks, Charlotte had been randomly inquiring about the inner workings of his drug operation. Charlotte was well aware of the fact that the FEDS were keeping the MFC members under surviallance. This didn't seem to detour her however and press was extremely impressed with her reseliance and display of resistance and fearlessness.

Press's maturity was outgrowing the developmental stages of his mind. This growth was highlighted once he started thinking of ways to run his businesss from prison. For him, this was the new goal. But at the same time, who could he trust enough within his organization to deal with Flores? Directly? Who would fill that void after today? Only one name seemed to come to mind. And it rhymed with wallet. Maybe she was the one for the job all along? Maybe that's what attracted them together. The suggested notion that they both like'd to live life on the edge. With press, it was never about the money. The adrenaline rush that was prescribed whenever he beat the judicial system is what kept him motivated. The hustle, money, and lavish lifestyle was a added bonus. Maybe Charlotte shared his same view's?

After all, Charlotte was an ex parole officer, so she probably had seen just as much police corruption as he did. Maybe, she would even be his successor, and eventually, inspire a rebellion, the same way he had.

Thinking about his lenient sentence, press stopped and smiled to himself. A twenty eight month prison sentence, in federal prison, was like coffee water, mixed with urine, inside of a toilet: it wasn't shit.

After deducting the four months credited for good time, six for the halfway house, and a additional nine for the drug program, press would probably serve only a small portion of his bid. Approximately eight months. If that.

Press had to pat himself on the back for humiliating the federal bureau all by himself. The more he thought about it, the bigger his ego got, almost replacing the size of the diamond inside of Charlotte's engagement ring.

"Excuse me sir. You dropped this," the little girl with the beads interupted, startling press. At this point he made it to his truck.

The little girl seemed to have pop up out of nowhere.

"Thanks," Press returned scanning the piece of paper that he was just handed by the little girl. It was a recpeit.

I probably dropped it outside of freidman's

"You look familiar. I'on kno—but ... press asked, more to himself. Do I kno you?"

"Ur Mr. Mcgurt?" The little girl inquired.

"Mmm-hmm."

"I attended one of the community centers. Before it closed."

"Which one?"

"Lincoln gym."

"O. Sho'll is. I remember you now. What are you doing way out here sweetheart? press returned, not really remembering her but genuinely concerned.

"Just on some business for my dad," the little girl explanied.

"All by yourself?"

Silence.

"You don't need to be way out here all by yourself babie girl. You to young to understand but theres plenty men out here that'll take advantage of you because of your age. It's called rape and child molestation," press coicered as he opened the driver sides door of his truck.

"Come on. Get in. I'm taking you home."

"How do I know your not one of those men?" the little girl sassed.

"Well, Press paused reaching for his information. That's the thing lil mama. You don't know. But here's my insurance policy, registration, and driver's license," he said as he pulled it out slow and handed it to her.

"So you can report me to the police if I misbehave."

Before closing the driver's side door, or receiving any response, press heard gun shots. Two of them.

BOOM! BOOM!

Hit, and shocked, Press tried his best to slam the car door but his pace wasn't fast enough. In seconds, two more bullets claimed the right side of his lung's, forcing him to curl up like a snail.

Somehow, press managed to crawl across the leather interior located in the inside of his vehicle landing directly on his back seat. Press maximized his strength's limit. Instinctively, he mashed the lock button on his keypad in an attempt to stop the intruder. But by this time it was to late because the shooter was already inside of his SUV with intentions to kill.

Feeling the barrel of the gun touch his forehead, Press said a silent prayer. He always knew that he'd die sooner or later. But not like this. He should've never got rid of his security he thought regretfully as moist drops of sweat filled his face.

What about his family? What kind of effect would his murder have on them? He wondered. And he didn't even want to think about his babie, Charlotte. Just the thought of her made him curse himself a million times for slipping so hard.

Stretched out on the back seat of his SUV, press stared his killer in the eyes. Press finally realized where he knew the little girl from. Back when he was a narcotic's agent, she was inside of the car with her dad, sabastian, a drug kingpin, and someone that his former colleages planted dope on. Because of the baseball cap she wore at the time, he mistook her for a boy. That's one of the reason's why he didn't recognize her. In fact, it was the same little girl who tried to fight him, the day he came to visit her mom on sabastian's behalf. He remembered because the same little girl had on a colorful t-shirt. In the center of it was betty boo's face. This landmark made it harder to forget because Charlotte's niece had the same shirt.

Never in a million years would press think that this same little girl would be a cold blooded killer. But she was. The gun pointed to his head was confirmation.

Nearing his last moments, Press closed his eyes and said another prayer as the little girl pulled the trigger. The impact from the gun caused his entire body to jerk.

Press ended up dying in the backseat of his own vehicle. The bullets from the gun carved the word Revenge right there in the center of his forehead.

EPILOGUE

Philo hopped out his lexus jeep in haste. He was furious while heading to see a particular person. Pissed, Philo entered the historical building. He failed to acknowledge the two-security guards that stood in the lobby to prevent unlawful entries. Security granted access, despite him having an attitude. A Mean mug was Philo's formal greeting.

Entering the office, Philo slammed the door behind him. The impact was so strong that it knocked a few pictures of the wall.

"Losing our patience are we my friend?" the mysterious guy (TMG) teased, faking a Spanish accent.

Philo replied by slamming his fist against the desk.

"What's with all the noise? Trying to start a marching-band?" TMG joked, sensing Philo's anger. He had been anticipating this very moment for the past twenty-four hours.

Instead of replying, Philo stared at TMG. His eyes were as fierce as a red devil.

"Ok. Fine. Enough jokes. You got the floor."

"My nephew was just murdered."

"Are you serious? When? Didn't he just get out based on that mistrial? He wasn't even home a week—*Fuck*

Fuck? That's all you gotta say to me? Fuck boy."

Fuck boy? TMG repeated in disbelief. Look. I'm sorry for your loss brotha. I really am. If there's anything I can do to help let me know," TMG added.

Philo snapped. "It was me who brought you into this organization. I put you in that position, you were a fuckin NOBODY. I was too good to you. You're blessed because of me. Thanks for rewarding me with treachery. The same mufucka that saved your life."

"Brotha. I understand what your going thru, trust me. You kno I do. Just kno that I got your back bro. Whoever did this will pay," TMG promised.

"I was doing fine running this city alone. When my superiors asked for my advice, I recommended you to be the face of this organization. They were looking to infiltrate law enforcement, so I provided them with a mole, which was supposed to be you, you selfish, disloyal, foolish, sonofabitch. Traidor."

"FUCC YOU MOTHAFUCKAAA. Philo yelled, ignoring TMG'S concern and generoisity. "TELL ME THE TRUTH. YOU OWE ME THAT MUCH. GODDAMMIT!!"

"YOU CAN'T HANDLE THE TRUTH!" TMG yelled back. He stood up and knocked two pictures off the wall the same way that philo did earlier. The picture frames contained pictures of his grandson.

"Wat? You need to hear me say-it? Okay. Fine, we'll play it your way then. Dear Philo. When it comes to your nephew, I hated his fuckin guts. So I had his punk ass murdered! HAPPY?" TMG yelled.

Philo rushed the mysterious guy swiftly, grabbing a hold to his body. They tussled for what seemed like forever knocking over tables, pictures, and numerous glass. Minutes later, a fleet of security guards then came running to break up the fight.

Screaming to the top of his lungs, Philo issued tons of threats before he was escorted out. It took almost ten guards to restrain him and place him in a choke hold.

After getting himself together, TMG picked up his phone and made a phone call. He had his grandson's birthday party to attend and he didn't have time to entertain the bullshit. Not now anyway.

After ending the call, TMG sat back behind his desk. Pictures, trash, and old documents were scattered all over the place. His office was a complete mess.

Thinking back to Philo's visit, TMG lit up a cuban cigar. For the past twenty years, him and Philo had developed an inseparable friendship. Their bond was like brothers almost. Only closer.

Traitor? Me? Tuh. I was the glue that held the organization together. That ship would've sunk a long time ago if it weren't for me. I saved your life as well, by keeping you out of jail. The generoisity extended equally. I was responsible for firing those agents and didn't even get a thank you. Yet I'm not complaining. Selifish my ass.

Philo ran the underworld for years without receiving a parking ticket. But This wouldn't be possible without TMG'S assistance. Philo thought the *UAT'S* influence and reach extended that far? That the FEDS would overlook the cartel's criminal behavior? How naive. TMG was the silent connection and link to the empire. He was responble for flooding the city with manipulation, drugs, and police corruption.

Philo's nephew was murdered because of a rumor. A rumor that a hit was placed on press by sabastian. This rumor was the center of all this confusion. And the reason why TMG was constantly angry and in deep thought.

No way in hell I was letting that slide. Mothafucker got exactly what he deserved. Hope he's burning like a bitch in hell too. He thought wrong if he thought that his newphew wasn't gonna suffer any consequences.

Grabbing his coat, TMG approached the door. Though the tension was suspended, he was still faced with the certainty of retaliation. At this piont, avoiding a confrontation with Philo was nearly impossible. Too many lines had been crossed and they were light-years past the point of no return.

Charlotte adjusted the ten-inch cake that sat firmly on her kitchen table. The cake contained a total of three candles, which represented the age of her son. Today, friends, family, and neighbors alike all came to help her celebrate.

Looking for her husband, Charlotte stepped to the patio in her very spacious backyard. Together, they were throwing a birth-day party and the two newly weds were its host.

"Preston McGurt the third. Boy, if you'on get down off that ban-ister," Charlotte threateneded, rushing to investigate. Out of all the kids who attended the party he was the baddest.

This little boy here is getting on my last nerve. If he keeps it up he can kiss his birthday party goodbye

After mumbling this to herself, and handling her son, charlotte looked outside and saw her husband. He was the celebration's or-ganizer and engaged into a conversation with Clarissa.

"When you get time, I need to see you," Charlotte mouthed si-lently once the two of them made eye contact.

After a few minutes passed, Ace stepped inside of the house. As soon as he saw charlotte he was confused.

"What's going on? He asked.

"I need you to go to the store to get some more barbecue sauce. We ran out."

"That it?"

"Umm-hmm."

"You sure? Because that mouth wash in the cabinet is calling your name. That breath is kicking like juan claud van *daaam.*"

"You so silly," Charlotte smiled, slapping Ace on his right shoul-der. Then she gave him a long passionate kiss.

It was crazy how life was charlotte thought. Never in a million years would she have thought that she'd marry Ace. For 1, their personalitites were complete opposites. For 2, that was press's confidant, predecessor, and first cousin. After press died, Char-lotte and Ace's bond continued to grow. During his stay in jail, she always went to visit him. When he was released, he came around to check on her periodically. Somewhere in the midst there was an attraction between the two, and out of nowhere, it just happened. It wasn't even planned. Casual sex sprouted to a relationship, and a relationship transcended into marriage. As it stood currently they were married for a total of six months.

They both felt like they were betraying press with their endeavors. But the family didn't seem to mind. "Who could help raise little press better than family? The gossiped went among one another. Eve was the only protester and she had no problem exhibiting her disgrace and disgust. This was the sole reason why she wasn't in attendance.

And speaking of the devil, eve was acting a fool these days while on the street of the seaport. Her and her jackboy/boyfriend, polo, had gotten back together and they were causing havoc all over the city of Savannah. Eve formed her own fraternity, which was in direct competiton with the MFC, which was now run by Ace, who was the one with the clout and dealing directly with flores.

Tandra hired some of the city's best attorneys to negotiate a better plea. After a variety of attempts, her legal team worked out a deal for forty-seven years instead of the life sentence. Eventually, charlotte also found out that Tandra was the one who ratted her out. The funny thing to charlottes was, it was actually tandra's own dope, which meant that she took the fall even tho she was innocent. At first, charlotte was highly upset, and hurt. But eventually, she forgave Tandra. After all, Tandra was the one in a federal prison somewhere in tim buck too, not her. So she needed as much sympathy as she could get. Ace, on the other hand, had a different take on his mother's betrayal, and he refused to send her money via money gram or western union. Charlotte felt like Ace was wrong and she often voiced her opinion on the issue. But ultimately, it was his mother, not hers, so she figured getting involved would be overstepping her boundaries.

On the way back to her living room, Charlotte caught a glimpse of her son. She had just wrapped up a conversation with one of friends and now she was admiring her son. He was handsome. And rebellious. Just like his dad.

Thinking back, charlotte remembered the last time that she saw press alive. They had just finished making love and she never got a chance to tell him that she was preganant with his child. She literally collapsed when she found out that he was killed. No-one even knew who did it. Although numerous suspects were targeted, namely the guy that everybody called Sabastian. The rumor was that he ordered the hit from prison.

Last week, sabastian was gunned down following his realease from prison, and she wondered if sabastian and press's murder was somehow connected.

Earlier, she spoke to Ace's uncle. He had promised to attend the party, adding that he was bringing a birthday present for little press. However, he sounded like he was upset about something tho charlotte suspected.

After everyting was settled, and everyone was present, they all gathered, including Ace. Soon, they'd be singing the happy birth-day song.

Charlotte was standing beside Ms. Rebbecca who was starting to become the family's surrogate grandmother since grandma McGurt had passed nearly a year ago. The seventy-eight-year old lady was questioning the children. She was going around in a circle asking them what they wanted to be when they grew up. Before this particular little girl even started her sentence, little press interjected. Ms. Rebecca hadn't even called upon him yet.

"When I grow up. I want to be just like my dad," little press the 3rd smiled, pointing his finger proudly at Ace, who stood atten-tively, not far away.

Shaking her head disappointingly, Ms. Rebecca wasn't surprised.

"I bet you do," she replied moving along to the next kid. She skipped the poor little girl for some reason. I bet you do," Ms. Re-becca repeated, as she called upon another one of the impatient children, who also blurted out of turn.

Attorney Valdez walked down the prison hallway after being instructed to do so. He couldn't stand the sight of prison, let alone visit one. But he had an important task today and this issue needed to be addressed immediately.

Entering his designated room, valdez sat down in a nearby chair and glanced at his client. The prisoner was shackled from head to toe. Gazing around the room, valdez saw a small video camera affixed to the ceiling.

"Matt. Lighten up some why don't cha. Geeeze. Whats with the evil look?" Attorney Valdez joked reavealing an Italian accent.

"I'm not in the mood to tolerate your sense of humor."

"Just chill man, chill. I'm not the bad guy here."

Silence

"Two of the internal affairs key witnesses recanted their testimonies. On top of that, two of those additional enhacements you received for reckless endangerment are challengeable."

"The only charge that leaves you with is the aggraved assault on that undercover cop. But you just about served that much of your sentence already."

After not getting the response that he was looking for, Attorney Valdez continued. "Now even tho we lost the appeal, we still have a fighting chance through filing this motion called a 2255. It's called a habeas corpus. Now the limitations on this motion are up because you were in prion for over a year. But we can file a successive 2255, because this would be considered new evidence," Attorney Valdez explained.

After going over everyting with his lawyer, Matt was led back to his corridor. He was confined in a federal FCI that held a capacity of approximately fifteen hundred inmates.

Thinking about his near future, a broad smile appearted on his big black face. His cornrows descended to his cheek bones, rubbing against the long scar he sported on the right side of his face.

"Valdez is full of shit" he mumbled. After all the money that valdez was given you'd think this news would've revealed itself visits ago.

During trial, the government witnesses were sheltered inside of the witness protection program. But that was then. Now it was different because Matt's people had finally caught up with them, which resulted in intimidation and the sudden change of heart.

Matt's prison sentence was finally coming to an end. And he was excited about that. But his morals were different now days. Now days his attitude towards the judicial system was as raunchy as ever.

This is the thanks I get? After all the shit that I did for the law enforcement community? I'll be home soon. Then its Fuck yall.

Matt's thoughts were interrupted by a new reality, *freedom*. Now, fuck the justice system was his attitude. This way of thinking was created by the internal affairs. Prison didn't change Matt. It only enhanced his greed, and rebellious state of conscienceness.

Today marked the beginning of a revolution. Hatred was becoming more and more of an necessity. It seemed as if a raging conflict between the government and the criminials was inevitable.

Knowing the information contained in the above paragraph, Matt formulated a devious plot following his attorney's departure. This time, he'd show the government who was boss, by murdering anyone that stood in his way, including dirtie cops.

It was only a matter of time before Matt was released from the federal bearu of prisons. And whenever that day did arrive, he'd show the world what it truly meant to *"Protect & Serve."*

———————